CABO
DE
GATA

Also available in English by Eugen Ruge

In Times of Fading Light

CABO
DE
GATA

a novel | **EUGEN
RUGE**

**Translated from the German
by Anthea Bell**

Graywolf Press

This publication is made possible, in part, by the voters of Minnesota through a Minnesota State Arts Board Operating Support grant, thanks to a legislative appropriation from the arts and cultural heritage fund, and through grants from the National Endowment for the Arts and the Wells Fargo Foundation Minnesota. Significant support has also been provided by Target, the McKnight Foundation, the Amazon Literary Partnership, and other generous contributions from foundations, corporations, and individuals. To these organizations and individuals we offer our heartfelt thanks.

Special funding for this title was provided by Edwin C. Cohen.

Published by Graywolf Press
250 Third Avenue North, Suite 600
Minneapolis, Minnesota 55401

www.graywolfpress.org

Published in the United States of America

ISBN 978-1-55597-757-3

2 4 6 8 9 7 5 3 1
First Graywolf Printing, 2016

Library of Congress Control Number: 2016931142

Cover design: Kyle G. Hunter

Cover art: Rivolto / Adobe Stock

For M.
I made up this story
so that I could tell it the way it was.

CABO
DE
GATA

I

Giving Notice

1

I remember stopping short midmovement. I remember the smell of coffee, or more precisely the smell of the little Arabian coffeepot I inherited from my mother, and what I specifically remember is how it smells inside when it's empty. I mean its own smell after it has brewed coffee hundreds and thousands of times (something I can describe only in rough-and-ready fashion by saying *metal* and *coffee grounds,* because usually I remember smells only when I'm actually smelling them).

As soon as I think of the coffeepot I remember the imprint of its ornamental brass handle on my left hand. But most clearly of all I remember the tiny (and probably pointless) movement of my hand when—*tack-tack!*—I tap the measuring spoon against the rim of the coffeepot and pause for a moment, maybe only a second.

I remember my surprise at suddenly finding myself there in my kitchen, in exactly that attitude, holding that coffeepot, in the middle of the tiny and probably pointless movement—*tack-tack!*—that I had carried out in just the same way the morning before (and the morning before the morning before), and for a moment I had the feeling that it was the *same* morning and I was the *same* man, a man who, like the undead, was doomed to repeat the same sequence again and again. The next moment I would go barefoot into the bathroom, as I had the morning before (and the morning before the morning before), I would have a cold shower, I would go back into the kitchen, still brushing my teeth, to turn down the gas when the coffee foamed up for the first time; I would stir my muesli—four kinds of cereal flakes with apple and banana—would make my way to my desk balancing the coffeepot in my left hand, and the muesli bowl on top of the coffee cup in my right hand, and I would switch on the PC while I began eating my muesli, hearing the fan start up with a sound like a spaceship, hearing the murmur of the hard disk, the eager clatter of the printer briefly testing itself and announcing that it was ready, and then, as on the morning before (and the morning before the morning before), I would sit in front of the screen, staring at the motionless blinking of the cursor, and I would know that, yet again, I wasn't going to get anything done today.

The next thing I remember is the moment when I tore off my old running pants and the cashmere pullover with holes in it (my favorite working clothes), and put on my jeans. I remember the stiff denim of the jeans, and the effort of forcing my body into them while it was still soft with sleep. I remember the despairing rage I felt, which in reality had nothing to do with the stiff fabric, but was the result of my casting my usual habits to the four winds. I was contravening an inescapable ritual, I was playing hooky from my self-imposed duty to work. My rage was vague and confused, but was directed chiefly against my father, as if it were his fault that I was reproducing, or imitating, his own regular, mechanical lifestyle, the way he sat down to work like a robot. The fact that it brought him success made it all the harder to bear.

I remember that a hot day was beginning outside, or rather I remember going down the corridor of the back part of the apartment, where I had been living since Karolin and I split up. I remember the cool air in the corridor and even now when, in my mind's eye, I pass the brightly painted front door of the punks who lived on the ground floor, I remember the smell of stale beer and marijuana and the lukewarm air blowing toward me through that ever-open door. I remember the penetrating heat of the sun outside the apartment building. I remember the brownish color of the asphalt. I remember that I was very soon sweating, because I was too warmly dressed, but most of all I remember the sweat cooling on my back and forehead as I sat in the Coal Café (in full, the People's Own Coal and Energy Café), in the shade of the large chestnut tree, perusing the breakfast menu.

I was the first customer. A waitress was going around with a small bowl, wiping down—a futile act—the garden furniture, which resembled bulky waste and which at the time, in the years of political change, I took for an interim solution, although it has now turned out to be a variant of the bohemian Prenzlauer Berg style in its own right. I forget what I ordered (some kind of Italian or Spanish or healthily organic breakfast), but I do remember that the waitress, who was probably studying business management or political science, addressed me by the formal *you* pronoun, and although I usually find it slightly intrusive to be addressed with too much informality in places like the Coal Café, the waitress's formality that morning annoyed me.

I don't remember the breakfast itself at all, or only the lettuce leaves that I didn't eat and the crumbs on the tabletop, and even those I recollect just because the sparrows set about pecking them up. I do know that I sat at the table for some time without moving, watching the sparrows. They approached cautiously but also with haste, their little claws slipping around on the tabletop as if they were novice skaters, and I also remember thinking it remarkable that even after thousands of years these birds, who after all had adapted superbly to city life, would probably never master the art of moving on a smooth tabletop without slipping off. It was simply beyond their capabilities, I reflected, but before I could pursue this train of thought any further the waitress came up to clear the table, shooing the sparrows away, and asked if I would like anything else.

Although my financial situation at the time was so precarious that before ordering every cup of coffee, I stopped to wonder whether I could afford it—or perhaps it was for that very reason, perhaps it was because I didn't want to look like a failure down on his luck to the obviously uninterested waitress—I ordered another *latte macchiato* anyway, and while I waited for my *latte macchiato,* something happened that I remember to this day in almost every detail.

Outside the café that had once been an ordinary coal merchant's place (and not, as the new owner from the Prenzlauer Berg district unwittingly supposed, a People's Own firm from East German days), a black BMW stopped and three men got out. They were young, or at least younger than I. Two of them wore short-sleeved T-shirts and jeans; the third was rather older than the others, looked more dissipated, and in general was what I imagined a pimp would be like. He wore a dark suit and a flowered shirt with its collar falling over the lapels of the suit jacket; a pair of presumably expensive sunglasses was perched in his mop of curly hair as if it had found its ultimate destination there; and he wore delicate shoes unsuited to any form of serious locomotion. They were moccasins, if that word is still in circulation, with two small strips of leather tied in a mock bow over the instep of each, the ends of the strips in turn forming tiny tassels.

In the "front yard" of the café, which in defiance of the regulations consisted of part of the broad Berlin sidewalk, commandeered for use by its customers, the seating was made up, among other things, of old planks that had once been part of some scaffolding and were now stacked along the wall of the building. They had probably been wiped down several hundred times by a waitress, but all the same they were covered with traces of whitewash and cement that had eaten into them. The suit wearer sat down on one of these planks without hesitating and began talking, in a loud Bavarian (or was it Austrian?) accent about things to do with computers. Or rather, he was talking about the sale of things to do with computers, about *market shares* and *expansion.* Words like *sales, marketing, percentage, profit margin,* and *franchising* (unknown to me at the time and still not entirely comprehensible today) assailed and penetrated my ear. The other two, more normally dressed men sat on plastic chairs turned to the speaker, bending slightly forward, nodding and making approving comments on what he said now and then, while the speaker himself, leaning back against the wall of the building, sat on the scaffolding plank with his legs crossed, letting an expression like that of a conqueror assessing what would shortly be his conquest travel over Kopenhagener Strasse, visible here for much of its length: over the gray facades, the windows, the rows of parked cars, and *all the time,* so my memory tells me, jiggling the foot of his crossed leg while the tassels of his ridiculous shoes, unsuitable for walking as they were, leaped around one another like dachshund puppies.

That, I think, was the moment when I conceived the idea of leaving this city (this country, this life) until further notice.

2

I recollect the sunny but already cool day in fall when I went to the mailbox. I was moving as if guided by remote control, or if my memory serves me correctly, like a man venturing into the street for the first time after a long sickness.

I also remember the letter dropping into the box, and the brief squeak of the flap. I remember that after mailing my letter I didn't go straight home but on along Gleimstrasse, past Falkplatz and toward the tunnel. The leaves of the maple (was it a maple?) on Falkplatz were already turning, the road led slightly downhill, and it could have been this downhill direction that reminded me of another occasion, several years earlier, when I had given notice before. Then I had not been giving notice of my intention to leave an apartment; I was giving notice at work, where I had a well-paid and of course permanent position at the Institute for Chemical Engineering. Even the fall of the Berlin Wall made no difference to that. The institute stood on a small rise called the Ravensberg, and now, as I walked past Falkplatz toward the Gleimstrasse Tunnel, I remembered going the long way from the Ravensberg down to the city on foot after a final conversation with the human resources officer. It had been fall then, too, with the sun shining, large, leathery leaves rustling underfoot, and the word *downhill* was haunting my mind like a prophecy.

Next I gave notice to the energy supplier and the telecommunications company. I recollect tedious phone conversations that went on and on, until one of the ever-changing people at the other end of the line agreed that I couldn't possibly be in possession of my own death certificate. That tiny detail may have been the deciding factor. I began searching my moving boxes, still not completely unpacked from last time, for other agreements, insurance policies, and so on, and although my haul can't have been particularly large I still seemed to be surprisingly deeply entangled in the whole thing (I mean society, the system), and the more difficult and laborious it subsequently became to extricate myself from that entanglement, the stronger my urge to do so became, until I was possessed by a positive mania for giving notice. I don't recollect in detail to whom I gave notice about what; I just gave notice to everyone and everything. I even succeeded in liberating myself from the medical insurance that every German citizen is legally bound to have, on the grounds that I would be out of the country for an indefinite period of time. But when I finally went to the residents' registration office, where oddly enough I had to produce written confirmation from my landlord before I could de-register, it turned out that to do so was possible only if I entered my future place of residence on the de-registration form.

I don't remember the woman's face anymore, only that she was a blonde (a bottle blonde). And I remember the aunt-like note of condescension in her voice as she said:

But surely you know where you're going.

I remember my attack of nausea when the first chocolate figures of Santa Claus appeared in shopwindows, and I still didn't know where I wanted to go. I remember the snowless darkness of the streets, the candy-wrapper luster of the shopping malls, the faces of the young women who seemed to me more unforthcoming than ever before in the artificial white light. And I remember the Advent star that was suddenly hanging everywhere in the stores, and although I am not a Christian, all at once I felt it was *intolerable* for that symbol to be so shamelessly exploited. I was even surprised that such a thing was allowed in this (allegedly) Christian country. I walked around among all these people buying and selling, full of resentment, and felt entirely confirmed in making my plans to flee.

But there were other moments, for instance, late afternoon, the only time of day when sunlight fell into my apartment. The light then was raspberry-red, seeming to thicken the air, and I drank it like syrup as I wandered barefoot around my two rooms; the little pendulum clock that I inherited from my mother made nibbling noises in its case like a pet animal, and I couldn't understand why I had given notice to leave the place.

I asked friends and acquaintances about their own experiences of foreign travel. I remember recommendations like South Africa or Ecuador. Ghana was also mentioned several times, and the Seychelles, of which I knew nothing at all. I do know I wondered how people had managed to travel far and wide so few years after the Wall came down. However, hardly anyone could think of a place that was warm in winter, at the same time inexpensive, and preferably could be reached traveling by land. I must admit that I hesitated to mention the last of those three conditions, because I didn't want to confess to discomfort at the prospect of flying, if not actual fear of it. Instead, remembering an entry in the Swiss author Max Frisch's diary, I said I liked to preserve a sense of the distance of the journey, or tried to explain that I didn't want either adventures or tourist attractions, which of course raised the question of what I did want—and I remember that I answered that question several times in very different ways, without feeling convinced of any of them myself.

In the end I went to the municipal library and studied climate maps. I remember red and blue diagrams, numbers and measurements, but what I remember with particular clarity is that I felt at more and more of a loss the more thoroughly I studied the subject—an experience that suddenly seemed to me familiar. The more closely I looked, the more blurred everything became. At this point, of course, Heisenberg's uncertainty principle occurred to me, and I entertained the admittedly philosophical rather than scientific idea that what Heisenberg described on the nuclear plane (to wit, the incomprehensibility in principle of the subject) is a quality immanent in the material, and one that consequently, indeed inevitably, must be continued in the visible world: *it was impossible for me to find the right place*. I liked this realization, and indeed it actually cheered rather than alarmed me. I remember that it felt as if I weren't taking my situation seriously, as if I were standing there studying myself like a character in a novel, and if I have remembered this moment of unfounded cheerfulness, like many other, less significant moments, then it is probably because at that time I was testing everything that I did or that happened to me at the same moment, or the next moment, or the moment after that, for its suitability as a subject—that even as I was living my life, I was beginning to describe it for the sake of experiment.

3

In a kind of weapons store I bought a supersharp Opinel knife (not stainless steel), and a small can of red-pepper spray. I also bought an inflatable neck pillow in Camp Four, for traveling at night, and a hammock that weighed almost nothing and took up very little space in my bag.

I knocked two strong hooks into walls of my room and slung the hammock between them to try it out. I had never used a hammock before. I remember that the word *embryonic* came into my mind as I tested it: embryonic passivity. Mother Earth taking me gently in her arms. I lay in the hammock for hours; I read in it, slept in it, used it as a chair where I sat to drink coffee. Lying in the hammock, I developed several theories that I remember only in vague outline: about the connection between idling and a sense of life (I mean the ability to feel that one is alive); about Columbus, who, as we know, brought the hammock to Europe; about ideas of growth and Christianity. I pictured myself and my hammock in fantastic southern landscapes, and suddenly everything struck me as easy. As long as there were two trees to support the hammock I would not be at a loss.

I remember sticking a note to my door: *sofa bed available free.* That afternoon there were two women at my door, both of whom I knew, although from different circumstances. I had already met one of them several times in the front hall of the building. She was not unattractive, slender, almost petite, and she always wore clothes that fitted her a little too tightly, but although—a year after my separation from Karolin—I hadn't been with another woman, although the physical proximity of women took my breath away, and I thought I could sense a feminine aura at arm's length, particularly indoors, I was surprised to find that I felt nothing when I happened to meet this petite woman on the stairs.

Beside her was a sturdy woman with a ring in her nose and a bald patch. I had seen her looking after the hairdressing salon on the corner, which was always empty, and had often wondered whether a hairdresser with a bald patch was the right advertisement for the salon.

They decided against my already rather stained sofa bed, but offered me twenty marks for the heavy black reading chair that once, even before Karolin's time, I had bought at an indecently high price from a secondhand furniture dealer. Although I had meant to store the chair in my father's cellar while I was away, I agreed to sell it, perhaps so as to make a start, perhaps because I was secretly glad that I would never have to drag the unwieldy chair up and down stairs anywhere again. When it came to moving it, however, I found myself involuntarily assuming the traditional masculine role. I took the chair from the petite woman— the woman with the bald patch was expecting her to carry the lower part of it—and with the half-bald woman I dragged it upstairs. Once there, before the petite woman, who had squeezed her way past us with difficulty, could reach a door and close it, I saw the explanation for the fact that while someone living above me seemed to have a dog, and regularly bawled it out, I had never seen the dog itself anywhere in the building: what I saw now was a cage, cubic and not quite large enough to hold a man or a woman, with—or so my memory tells me—chains, handcuffs, and paddles like fly swatters hanging from its bars.

I decided to leave the rest of my things (apart from my computer, my mother's clock, the crate of documents and books, and the Arabian coffeepot) to the punks on the ground floor—although I had suspected them for some time of stealing my bicycle. It was afternoon when I rang their bell. After a long time a dozy character with a badly squashed Mohican hairstyle opened the door. In an ominously bad temper, he accompanied me up three floors, inspected my sofa bed, my Ivar shelving, my desk, which consisted of a laminated wooden board, my two chairs, my three-piece 1950s wardrobe, and the cutlery cabinet complete with contents that I had bought in a junk shop, and then said it would cost me to get rid of this lot. I said I'd think about it.

In fact, however, I borrowed my father's car, which as usual was problematic because my father was one of those men who, as products of their generation, held that you should never lend "cars, women, or shavers" (all enumerated in a single breath) to anyone else. I took apart the shelves and the wardrobe, dragged it all downstairs, carted the bulky stuff away to the Berlin Municipal Cleansing Department, and threw the rest in the apartment building's garbage container. I don't know why I didn't ask anyone to help me, but I know that I didn't. I remember maneuvering the steel frame of my sofa bed, sweating and cursing, down the winding stairwell, and I remember breaking the cutlery cabinet apart in the inner courtyard so that nothing would fall into the hands of the punks when I had moved out.

I drove off to my father's place with the rest of the stuff in his car.

4

After my mother's death my father had moved to a smaller apartment. His new cellar also turned out to be small, in fact, really just a cubbyhole, and I remember that after I had filled it with my things my father came down and inspected it. How long was all this going to be left here, he asked, as his eyes passed over my boxes and bags. I murmured something about a few months. Almost imperceptibly my father shook his head, and I remember (or am I just imagining that, because it would have been so typical of my father?) how his eyebrow rose—the right eyebrow, or maybe it was the left—and stayed raised as he turned to the cellar steps again.

Later we sat in a room that he had furnished just like his old one in every detail. My father asked the usual questions, and I answered them in the usual way. I don't remember exactly what he asked, but one of his typical questions was: *How is the world of art doing?* although he didn't think that what I had done since giving notice to the institute counted as art; my radio features, for instance, only two of which, so far as I remember, he had ever heard, one about church windows in Brandenburg, and another, which was really very funny, about a writer who made her living by writing the biographies of cats and dogs as commissioned by their respective owners. Of course I hadn't told him that I intended to write a novel, and I wasn't going to, because he thought anything later than the great realists of the nineteenth century was either superfluous or at least questionable.

He considered his own activities far more important than mine. Even at the age of seventy, he was still writing articles on the history of philosophy for newspapers that paid no fee. They were always about the great European revolutions, *questions of humanity,* as he put it. That day he talked about an article on the July Revolution of 1830 in France that had just appeared somewhere, casually and critically, as always tacitly assuming that everyone was familiar with the historical background to his article, so yet again—and this is what I really remember—I seemed to myself rather dull-witted.

From here he went on, as usual, to the international situation as a whole, and finally, after expressing his abhorrence and contempt for everything going on in the world in general, almost more by dint of volume and gestures than words, he ended up as if following a set pattern with the GDR, or more precisely the former GDR, or the new Federal German provinces, as they were now called, attacking the usual conspiracy theories. In this case he was talking about some kind of examination that was to be made of pensions, in his opinion serving solely to reduce his own pension because he had been a former member of the Socialist Unity Party. I also remember that we quarreled about it, and yet again I failed to say what really annoyed me about the matter, which was that fundamentally he was among the beneficiaries of the fall of the Wall, for while his younger colleagues were competing to get work on short-term projects, or were unemployed, or opening sausage stalls and travel bureaus, the crucial timing of the change of regime had caught him just at retirement age, so he now drew a good pension from the hated West German republic, and if it was not quite as much as a professor emeritus from the West got, he did have a monthly salary that far exceeded my own average income. That, it seemed to me, made it easy for him to feel important—even if no one actually paid for the articles he wrote.

All the same, he gave me a thousand marks by way of "Christmas money," as always incidentally and without comment, for although he still thought it unpardonably stupid of me to have left the institute, he was sensitive enough not to accompany the generous financial presents he gave me from time to time with implied criticism (for which I am still grateful to him). Up to this point in our meeting all had been the same as before, that's to say, as it was in my mother's lifetime. Our conversations and arguments were the same, even the room where we were sitting looked the same, and I had to take care not to feel as if my mother had only just gone into the kitchen and would soon be calling us into the living room to eat.

Of course she didn't, and I asked my father in passing, already halfway to the kitchen, whether I could make myself a sandwich, but it turned out that my father had already literally *counted* the slices of bread—it was some kind of ready-sliced supermarket loaf with a strong sorbic acid content so that it would keep. It was the weekend, he pointed out, and well, he had a visitor coming tomorrow . . .

I remember my father rocking from foot to foot, I remember his face, tense with embarrassment. I think now that his embarrassment could have been because the visitor was a lady, but at the time I assumed he was ashamed of counting the slices of bread, and my father—my ever superior, cool, and composed father, the raconteur and man of the world, the great orator and famous author—turned before my eyes into a lonely old man counting slices of bread to see how many he had left. And instead of laughing at him for this persnickety counting of crumbs, as he himself would have described it, I murmured something by way of changing the subject and even reassuring him, so disturbed was I by suddenly feeling sorry for my father.

It must have been on the following night that I dreamed my mother rose from the dead. I made a note of the dream at the time, as I do with all my dreams, but—for some reason even I don't entirely understand—in writing this down I have decided not to look at any earlier accounts, nothing to refresh my memory or inspire me, not to look anything up on Google or in Wikipedia or, which would have been easy, to revisit the place where the cat finally met me. I will rely on those oscillations of the mind that we call memory. One of them shows me an image of my mother.

I see her coming from the graveyard, indeed still in the graveyard but on her way home; she is in a kind of intermediate stage, wearing the white dress in which she was buried, but I can sense (even from a distance) the warmth slowly returning under her skin. She looks as if she has slept well; her red hair is untidy. She pushes a strand of it back from her face, doesn't make much of the entire incident; she just wants to go back to ordinary life, tidying up the apartment, shopping, cooking, but my father runs back and forth in front of her, in great agitation, explaining why none of that is possible. He has, he argues, taken care of all the formalities, he has acquired all the medical certificates, all the legal stamps on the documents; her place in the graveyard was paid for twenty-five years in advance, and my mother, he thinks, can't expect him to cancel all that out (also, as I sense, after sending everyone her death announcement, he would feel awkward about explaining now that it was all a mistake). In short, he objects in no uncertain terms to her resurrection—and my mother lies down in her grave again.

5

I don't recall that Christmas now, but I do remember New Year's Eve.

It was my last night in Berlin, and I had really meant to go to a party given by a friend of mine, or more precisely a former friend, for under the new regime he had set up as *self-employed* (self-employed as what I don't know to this day; all I knew about it was that he was always preparing *presentations* of some kind and was constantly short of time), and since he became self-employed the contact between us had gradually slackened off. Now he and some other self-employed people were having a large party on a factory floor, three hundred guests, almost all of whom, as I realized, would be strangers to me— in fact, exactly the kind of event I normally avoid. This time, however, I had decided to go, to disappear, to give myself the deceptive feeling of being among other human beings. But then Karolin called and asked me if I would like to take Sarah out. The child was longing to see me, she said.

I remember that telephone conversation very well. As usual it was fragile and threatened to break off at any moment. Karolin wasn't begging but *asking* me, and any hesitation would have led to the withdrawal of the question, leaving me with uneasy feelings. Karolin was very good at making one feel uneasy. She never said anything straight out, but now that I think about the message hidden behind her shy attitude on that occasion, it ran like this: after all, she's not your daughter, she seemed to want to point out to me, and if you don't want any more to do with her that's your right—and immediately I would suspect myself of seeing the child all this time only as a last way of making contact with her, Karolin; above all, I would secretly have welcomed the fact that Karolin still hadn't brought herself to enlighten her daughter about the matter of her paternity because I thought it allowed me to think our relationship might still have a chance—while the child, as it turned out, was *longing to see me.*

But at the very moment when Karolin opened the door, with a towel around her head and in a bathrobe that she had thrown on hastily, showing a glimpse of black stockings underneath—at that moment I realized that she wanted to be rid of the child on New Year's Eve only because she had decided to throw herself at some man or other, the way she had thrown herself at me—heroically but also antisocially; it's difficult or perhaps just embarrassing to explain what had drawn me to Karolin in the first place: the lipstick that was rather too bright on her bleary-eyed face, her sore feet in brutally high heels, her determination verging on self-denial.

Sarah was standing in the corridor, surprisingly tall, it seemed to me, when I hadn't seen her for several weeks. She was quiet, shy, hardly ventured to look at me, and I felt unwell as I leaned down and said a few kind words to her. I felt unwell because of Karolin's proximity, the smell of the apartment, the sight of the old sofa on which—and on our first evening at that—she had brought me to ejaculation with her freshly painted lips. I watched as Karolin put a jacket on the slightly reluctant child, slung a school backpack containing something around her shoulders; as she bent down I saw her small breasts, slightly slack after pregnancy and breast-feeding, which at that moment seemed to me immensely desirable—until Karolin pulled the lapels of her bathrobe together as if reading my thoughts.

Sarah and I went to the newly opened fish and seafood restaurant of the Nordsee chain and ordered the English dish of fish and chips (Sarah wanted it mainly for the chips; I got to eat most of her fish). Then we went to the cinema and saw some kind of animated cartoon. I didn't take in much of it because I kept thinking of how Karolin would be spending the evening; I imagined her doing everything we used to do together with some other and, as I instinctively assumed, rich guy, an attorney from Düsseldorf or a designer from Munich; I imagined her, after they had been dancing all evening, holding each other close, whispering silly things into one another's ears, taking him home with her at two in the morning, putting a steak in the pan for him, sitting opposite him with her feet up and her thighs pressed together as she gazed at him with adoration.

I was afraid that Sarah might be bored in my empty apartment, so I had bought all the necessary ingredients for making baked apples with vanilla sauce, but the child was in transports of delight to find that she was allowed to draw on the walls with the colored pens she had brought in her bag, and I was left alone with my baked apples in the kitchen, cracking nuts with an old chisel and coring apples, while Sarah had only to stir the vanilla sauce in my one remaining pan, and only now, in my surprise at seeing that she knew how to do it even without looking at the instructions on the packet, did I realize that she was beginning to turn into a woman—and I would lose not only Karolin but Sarah too. Soon she would discover that I was not her father. Soon Karolin would be in a stable relationship again, might even marry (earlier, when she'd still had hopes for me, she had always been wanting us to get married), would go to Düsseldorf or Munich or heaven knows where, maybe America—that was the way my thoughts were running—and someday, I imagined, a tall, dark beauty would meet me in the street and cast me, a man much too old for her, a surreptitious glance, and only when she had gone past would I understand why that young woman had looked at me . . . But guess what, here my memory deceives me, for the dark beauty that I think I remember imagining is exactly like today's Sarah, and at that time, after all, I can hardly have known what Sarah would look like in the future.

Later we lay on the floor, both of us reverting to childhood, and using shoes and socks, colored pencils, handkerchiefs, and anything else we could lay hands on we improvised an imaginary fairy tale, with an absurd plot full of dramatically unjustified twists and turns. I don't know now what it was about (it had something to do with

Chinese opera but also with garbage disposal, and a creature that had been accidentally thrown away and whom we called Three-Gram-Kvowch), but I do remember that I found myself going with the flow as I made up his story; suddenly I seemed to be free of all the pedantic and compulsive, reserved and secretive qualities that I regarded as my inheritance from my father, and that I was sure were an obstacle to me in real life as well as in my writing.

At midnight we went up on the roof to see the fireworks with which Berlin was welcoming in the New Year. I remember that the two lesbians were among the people standing on the roof, and they called out "Happy New Year" to me, with emphasis on the *New.* I remember the occasional, heavy flakes of snow that you didn't see in the darkness above the rooftops, but felt only when they touched you. I remember Sarah's cheeks, shining with the moisture, and the happiness in her face. And I remember the sense of confidence that came over me, the almost forgotten, youthful confidence that once—how long ago was it?—had carried me through life like a guardian angel.

The next day I boarded a train for Barcelona.

6

Or rather, I boarded a train for Basel, where I was going to catch the night train to Barcelona. At the station's information desk, I had been told that was the simplest and cheapest way of going south, and south was where I wanted to go.

Before the train left the Berlin East railroad station, I had bought a little Spanish–German dictionary and a travel guide, rather out of date and therefore at a reduced price, and by doing so I nearly missed the train. It was one of the high-speed trains that were new at the time. It started without a jolt, and when today, traveling first-class, I regularly complain to the entirely blameless conductors about the growling, howling noise to be heard at certain speeds, I must admit that at the time the train seemed to make no sound at all—although all I recollect is the slow journey through Berlin, which rolled by, out of reach beyond the hermetically sealed windows, and although I saw only the typical areas of wasteland beside the ballast on the tracks, the power lines, the allotments, the garden sheds, I do remember that at the sight of them I felt a lump in my throat.

All I know about Basel is that I was standing on the platform there late in the evening, listening to an announcement in three languages (as far as I remember), delivered in a routine female voice that echoed from the roof of the station concourse, sounding as far away and scratchy as if it came from a radio receiver of the past.

While I understood almost nothing of the announcement, I still remember perfectly the first two Spanish words I heard spoken by a human being, namely, the conductor of the night train, who initiated me into the workings of the electrically adjustable reclining seat. *Bajo,* he said as he pressed a button to move the seat down, and *alto* as he brought it up again. I inflated my neck cushion and pressed *bajo*.

The next image I see is from the following morning: the train is chugging along at a slower speed through unattractive suburbs. Shabby new, pink buildings, reminiscent of Romania or Russia. I notice, hopefully, that the inhabitants leave their potted plants out on the balconies here even in January.

Then I see myself going down a long avenue lined with palm trees. I almost seem to feel the rucksack containing what remains of my life on my shoulders, while my legs remember the weight of it. I was walking at a slow and regular pace—and if I linger on that image a little longer, I even remember that because I was bending under my burden and my hat obscured my vision, I tried to push it back, which proved difficult on account of the way the brim knocked against the rucksack that rose up behind me.

I went to the Plaza de Colón—a round space with a column in it, and on top of the column Columbus indicating the sea with a wide-ranging gesture (although I thought he was looking the wrong way, namely, southward)—and then I turned right into the Rambla to look, in the next intersecting street or the one after that, for the little hotel recommended as good value in the Spanish travel guide that I had bought at the station in Berlin. I think it was called the Hotel Maritim, and was on the second or third floor of a showy, late nineteenth-century building. On the other side of its equally showy door, I found a kind of reception desk, really only a counter, where a stout middle-aged man seemed to be eking out his existence. His face was the color of plant shoots that don't get enough daylight, his movements were sinuous, and to my ears his Spanish sounded like water running down a drain. He showed me a dark, narrow room that on closer inspection turned out to be part of what had once been a larger room, now divided by a plywood partition. You could see the abrupt break in the stucco molding on the ceiling. The room cost fifteen hundred pesetas, about eighteen marks a night, and I remember that I immediately began calculating how long my money would last if I stayed here.

After putting down my rucksack, I went out into the Rambla again. It must have been about ten in the morning. The sun was warming up, the sky was blue. I felt wonderfully unburdened without my rucksack. I had read in the travel guide that the beautiful word *rambla* originally meant a dried-up riverbed, and I still remember that this little etymological turn of phrase instantly helped me to get my bearings, and feel that I knew a little about the topography of the city center that seemed to have grown up round this former riverbed.

As I do in every strange city, I immediately began to look for what was special and out of the ordinary in the scene before me, what made it typical of Barcelona. I remember the many newspaper kiosks opening up as I passed them, one after another, like gigantic butterflies spreading their wings as they emerge from the cocoon. I remember women selling flowers who were beginning to set out their wares on the sidewalk, and farmers' wives stacking cages containing live chickens on top of each other. I remember a blind man selling lottery tickets sitting amid this colorful show in a little booth no bigger than a telephone box, feeling the bill proffered by a woman customer with both his thumbs and his two forefingers.

I had also read in the travel guide that here, on the paving of the Rambla, there was a mosaic by Miró, and although I must admit that my interest in Miró was only moderate I began looking for it, at first casually and then with increasing restlessness. I went back and forth several times between the Plaza de Colón and the Plaza de Cataluña, but the likelihood of finding the Miró grew less and less. Every time the paved surface of the road was increasingly occupied, the Rambla was fuller and the crowds larger. Suddenly there were stalls everywhere, selling various kinds of junk: items sold as souvenirs, textiles probably made in Vietnam, and after I had passed, several times, one of the carpets of flowers laid out on the road, I knelt down and promptly found my suspicion confirmed: the flowers had no scent.

I left the Rambla, walked through the Old Town for a while, looked at several of the so-called sights of the place, of which I remember no more, and really not even that I saw them. I do clearly remember, however, the blind lottery-ticket sellers, who were suddenly everywhere, and who now looked to me like slaves of some mighty criminal organization, and I remember the restlessness impelling me, as if it sprang from my unsuccessful search for the Miró mosaic, taking me through the old streets and alleys as if I were still looking for something. I went into a restaurant near the market hall and ate *bacalao,* apparently a national dish: salt fish in a dark sauce thickened with a roux. After that I sat on a bench and slept in the sun for an hour. Then I set off again—this time to Gaudí's cathedral, the largest and most famous in Barcelona, on which, as the travel guide boasted with curious pride, building has been in progress for over a hundred years because it is financed solely by donations and grants from various foundations.

I don't remember now whether the cathedral was closed, or whether I was feeling too stingy to pay the entrance fee if there was one, but anyway I saw only the exterior of the building: a monstrous pile that I circled several times, amazed to see such lunacy made stone. Six, seven, or eight towers stabbed the silken evening sky like spears. A homeless woman was settling down for the night in the gardens at the back of the cathedral.

I had gone a few stations on the Metro, and made the return journey on foot, still looking for—for what? My travel guide recommended the discotheques of Barcelona, spoke of "the hottest mile in Spain," and I do recollect cellar entrances illuminated in shades of red, green, and blue, with music pulsing out of them. I remember that I passed by without stopping: even then, when I was only just over forty, I felt too old for such places, and feared the eyes of young women looking straight through me, bearing their youth aloft like something that did them personal credit, and I feared the comparison with serious young men wearing black-rimmed glasses, and running their fingers thoughtfully through gleaming dark hair.

After a while I found myself back on the Rambla. Night had fallen. The moon had risen in the sky—a waxing moon, if I am not mistaken. A cold wind was blowing. The Rambla was empty. Only the newspaper kiosks, now folded down, were still loitering in the street, shadowy boxes on wheels distributed all over the Rambla, and just before the Plaza de Colón, in front of a brightly lit sex shop on the other side of the road, several prostitutes stood in a tight circle like animals in search of warmth. I noticed one of them in particular, although I could see her only from behind. She was a tall blonde wearing a short, blue, fake-fur jacket sprinkled with hundreds of little silver stars, and a skirt, also blue, beneath which I could see her long, shapely legs, made to look even longer by the tapering high heels of her shoes and the black seams of her stockings.

The women didn't notice me until, giving them a wide berth as I walked around them, I slunk into the sex shop, and I remember clearly how absurd and indeed morbid it seemed to me that I was bypassing these living creatures on my way to see something dead and fleshless. Presumably I remember my brief visit to the video cabin only because, in glancing through the program on offer, I really did come upon something unusual, out of the ordinary, or at least that I had never seen before, a film in which two women in colorful garter belts were busy with the private parts of a—was it a donkey or a mule? Then the film ended because I didn't put a coin into it.

I also remember that I stayed sitting in the cabin for a while. The soles of my feet were sore. Music of no specific origin reached my ears from a neighboring cabin, interspersed with muted moans. As I left the sex shop the women who had been standing in a circle before had moved here and there in the street, and the woman in the blue fur jacket with the beautiful long legs was now standing alone in front of the shop, this time turned toward me.

I looked at her and realized that I was looking into the face of a woman of seventy.

7

I slept badly that night because of the cold. The bed was made in a way that I would now describe as Mediterranean. There was only a thin and, I suspected, grubby blanket wrapped in a large sheet. I remember that as I dropped off to sleep I was anxious not to come into contact with the blanket, instead of getting up and taking my sleeping bag out of my rucksack.

I woke much too early, my limbs stiff with cold.

There was no breakfast available in the hotel—or really *hostal*—but the pale receptionist, who had not seemed either particularly welcoming or particularly voluble the day before, suddenly and effusively waxed loquacious and recommended a certain café, even got me to repeat his (very simple) directions for finding it, and called its name after me several times, so it would have seemed very meanminded of me not to accept his recommendation.

The café was at the southern end of the Rambla, just before the Plaza de Colón, where the street begins to grow wider like the mouth of a river. I think I was the first customer, although the interior seemed to be buzzing with activity. Two bartenders, one of them polishing glasses, the other cleaning the espresso machine (or some other piece of mechanical equipment), stood behind the counter. In front of it several waiters had positioned themselves in wine-red liveries that looked rather worn out, joking and talking to each other, but all drawn up in rank and file as if at an invisible starting line. Napkins over their forearms, they seemed to be expecting customers to burst in at any moment.

I put my rucksack down and found a table beside a floor-length window with a view of the plaza beyond.

I don't remember exactly when I decided to leave Barcelona again that day, but I had certainly come to that decision when I sat down there, and I remember being surprised to find how much my perceptions had changed in view of it, and that after examining this change in my usual way it seemed to me worth describing: the fact that I simply accepted the wrong sort of croissant when the stout, bald waiter brought it over; that on the other hand I found it almost touching that after he had put down my large cup of white coffee he pushed the plate a little closer to me with both hands, as if he must encourage me to eat; that neither the gurgling of the espresso machine, drowning out the voices of the regular customers as they talked to the bartender while they drank their coffee standing; nor even the fact that the garbage truck was left standing outside the door with its engine running, so with the arrival of everyone who came in, a blast of cold morning air mingled with diesel fumes also entered the café—none of this disturbed me.

I spent all morning in the café. The sun rose beyond the plaza, a white disk behind opaque glass clouds, gradually gathering strength and warming my frozen limbs. Traffic began circulating around the column with Columbus on it. A waiter was putting aluminum chairs down on the sidewalk outside my window with much clinking, and I saw several young women who looked very busy tripping past outside, all of them, it struck me, wearing high-heeled shoes and opaque brown pantyhose. I also noticed something else: they were all carrying papers or documents openly under their arms, like architects on a building site or people who come to read the electricity meter, so I speculated on the conclusions that might be drawn from their ostentatious disregard for briefcases or college bags regarding the probability of rain in this region.

After a while three or four construction workers came along, closed off the other side of the street, and began breaking up the asphalt with a jackhammer, an endless, monotonous process, and as I watched and heard the old city rousing itself and getting ready to face the new day, whatever it cost, I suddenly thought of the old prostitute yesterday evening, who was now, one could assume, also preparing to face the day, rousing herself after a cold night spent standing around on high heels, and, before she went to buy food for a meager breakfast in the supermarket, carrying out emergency repairs to her face and figure in the bathroom mirror, or brewing coffee—I imagined her cutting short the time that would take by using water already heated by the boiler—anyway, I think I remember that that was what I imagined, although I may be thinking up a new image, for fundamentally memory reinvents all memories, and maybe my image of the prostitute filling her mini-boiler from a small boiler hanging over the sink, making it so to speak the invention of an invention, which may be deduced from the fact that I had been thinking about this point. However, what I really do know—to risk that word again—is that in the café that morning I thought up a name to bestow on her, or rather not to bestow on her but one that, I suddenly thought, was rightfully hers: I thought she was Miss Barcelona in person.

Then the stout waiter brought a newspaper in a holder to my table, some kind of tabloid with a wealth of pictures and few words, such as I wouldn't even have glanced at in Germany, but the waiter's thoughtfulness, his encouraging nod, the fact that although the café was now full he wasn't trying to get rid of me, but even brought a newspaper to my table, resulted in my ordering a second (or third) cup of white coffee, and leafing through the newspaper at least for the look of the thing, even though my Spanish wasn't even up to the level of a large-circulation tabloid. Somewhere, maybe on the front page, I found a weather forecast that I understood, because it basically took the form of a map. A spectrum of color from blue to orange showed the distribution of warm weather on the Spanish mainland, and in sketch maps on the Mediterranean islands, and the brightest orange patch was on the southeast corner of the country, around a place called—I didn't really know whether it applied to the region as a whole or a particular place—called Cabo de Gata.

8

Now, as I sit in the plane on my way from Minneapolis to Tokyo fifteen years and a millennium later, typing these sentences on the laptop on my knees, it seems to me unlikely, as if it were something made up after the event, that at the time I didn't know what *Andalusia* was.

Similarly, I hardly remember what I felt when I looked up Cabo de Gata in my travel guide, and found it listed as a place in the southeast of Andalusia, which may be because I immediately suppressed the embarrassing discovery that Andalusia was a landscape that really existed.

Because a few years earlier, in the days of the German Democratic Republic, I had been to see Buñuel's famous film *An Andalusian Dog*. I have almost no recollection of the film itself—I can excuse myself by saying that the circumstances in which I saw it were extremely trying. We were in a more or less illegal club cellar in East Berlin, the film was showing in its original language, and if it had any subtitles they were in English; it broke off several times during the performance and I am not even sure whether I saw it to the end or whether, unnerved by the constant pauses, the cold, and the ponderous aesthetic, which aimed to reeducate the audience, I left the club cellar before it was over or spent parts of the showing in the bar just above it, smoking. What I do remember, however, is the impression left on me by the title of the film, which I probably remembered so well because I did not entirely understand it. I did not connect the word *Andalusian* with geography in any way, but thought it a kind of fantastic adjective meaning "wonderful" or "enchanting," something like that. Andalusia not only sounded strange and far away, like the names of all those places that lay out of reach behind the Iron Curtain; it was, I thought, a fairy-tale place, an invention—until I saw it on the weather map of that Spanish newspaper, and then, when I read in my travel guide that Cabo de Gata was "the last romantic fishing village" in Andalusia, where the boats, said the guide, were "still brought up out of the water with a hand winch," when I read that in the national park of Cabo de Gata you already felt "a breath of Africa," I realized that this was the place I had been looking for.

I caught the overnight bus. I remember a terrible journey. Presumably the bus driver turned off the constant video streaming at some point, but a never-ending film haunts my memory, an inescapable torture. Its images still come back to me as reflections from the dark windows, shots, noises, screams, entering my defenseless ears and getting into my brain. I am sitting hunched in my seat, hating my fellow travelers for putting up with these torments, even apparently welcoming them. Once we stopped in a village, of which all I remember is an unplastered, rectangular house in the light of a streetlamp. Then we drove through a landscape on which the first gray light of morning fell, treeless, hilly, bleak, and I remember how, in defiance of all probability, I said under my breath to the window, to myself, *I am in Andalusia.*

Next was the bus station in Almería, a miserable and if I remember correctly pink concrete building. I see no more of Almería. My travel guide has told me the city is hardly worth a visit. The only thing that interests me here is how to get away from it. There seems to be a connection by bus to my destination, and I still have time for a sandwich and coffee. Then a rickety bus drives up with a notice behind the windshield: *Cabo de Gata.*

I ask the bus driver how long the drive takes; I hope it will be quite a long way, because what I have seen so far is not exactly what I would expect "a breath of Africa" to feel like. I laboriously compose my question. But the bus driver, a fat man in a dirty, reddish-brown cardigan, does not even turn to look at me, only lets out a hissing sound through the gaps in his front teeth. I ask the man a second time, but again he only hisses, and when I venture to say that I still haven't understood him, he suddenly turns a quarter of the way around, rises a little way from his seat, propping his hands on the steering wheel, and, obviously annoyed by the trouble he has to go to on my account, he says, loud and clear, failing to pronounce the letter *s, TRE ORA!*

He laughs, and suddenly turns to the three or four other passengers, to make sure they have all heard his joke—but what exactly was the joke?

The bus starts before I can sit down. I stagger along the central aisle, flung back and forth between the seats. One of the passengers who was laughing at me just now thinks he can reassure me by telling me the real length of the journey in a whisper, *Cuarenta y cinco,* forty-five minutes. I sit down, look out the window, wait for what is going past outside it to begin having a breath of Africa about it.

I remember the wretched (pink) buildings in the background; it is hard to say whether they are still being built or already falling into ruins. I remember primitive suburban houses, their roofs so low I can look down on them from the bus. I also remember mended stretches of tarmac, black water containers, antennae, tangles of cables. I remember a tiny garden café with dusty chains of colored lights. I still vividly remember the palm tree at the side of the road, a gray and also dusty thing managing, somehow, to live in ground that is as hard as concrete.

Then the town comes to an end. The bus, in a complicated looping movement, swings toward an elaborate road junction that links two almost deserted narrow country roads in the middle of the desert here—swings around in confusing curves, only to end by going straight ahead.

I remember positive hills of garbage to the right and left of the road. Builders' rubble, broken paving stones, rocks all piled up, a garbage heap with a few weeds growing on it. The whole landscape looks to me like a sparsely overgrown dump. As far as I can see there are broken shards, old shoes once I see the framework of a child's stroller; and again and again the achievements of the polymer chemicals industry spring colorfully to the eye, hardly weathered at all because of their ability to withstand acid and lye. In a hundred years' time these yellow plastic bags will still be fluttering in the wind, caught on the spines of agave plants.

We are about halfway when I see a huge notice by the roadside. I hardly need my dictionary to translate it. All the same I look it up, because I don't believe what the notice says:

PARQUE NACIONAL CABO DE GATA—
EL ÚLTIMO PARAÍSO DE EUROPA

From then on I begin to count the remaining minutes before we reach Paradise.

9

I don't remember seeing any place-name on display as we enter the village. The bus jolts over the edge of a curb and comes to a halt. I am the last passenger. The bus driver opens the door and calls out something without turning around. Then I am standing in a square, or more precisely in a triangular area with sharp angles between two streets leading into a traffic circle. The ground is dry and crusted. A ramshackle wall marks off the segment. There is a transformer hut. A rusty bus stop stands askew, the timetable stuck to it now illegible as a result of the sun and the sea air.

The bus jolts back over the curb and into the road, and is gone.

I shoulder my rucksack and make for where I think the sea must lie. A dog, a husky, lies asleep outside a small supermarket. There is a small church to the left, a raised area to the right. A row of tiny, two-story apartments—all deserted.

After about three hundred meters I come upon the beach promenade. Although keen gusts of wind are raising sand from the ground and blowing it into my eyes, the sea moves lazily, a regular expanse of gray reaching to the horizon, where it merges directly with the sky.

I slowly walk along the promenade. Dogs surround me, yapping at me: small brown-and-white mongrels, all looking exactly the same.

The buildings along the promenade look the same as those in the rest of the village: cubes in pastel colors, all caught between waiting to be finished and beginning to fall down. Only one of the three restaurants on the promenade is open, or rather the grating over the entrance is only half-closed. The glazed door is swinging in the wind.

I remember a large room with tiles reaching halfway up its walls (in an ornamental pattern that I would describe as Moorish). The only windows are on the same wall as the door. The light is dimmer the farther you go into the room. I remember assuming that the old woman who emerges from the dark background must be the cleaning lady. *Buenos días,* she says, or rather *Bueno día,* because here, too, the letter s is not pronounced. With the bus driver I put it down to his missing front teeth, but this woman still has all her teeth—or I should perhaps say has them all back again, because her white, regular dentition does not suit her earth-colored, wrinkled face, nor does her large pair of glasses seem right for her face, nor does the chestnut-brown hair set in rigid waves on her head.

I sit at the bar and order coffee. There is a brief rattle from the espresso machine, and then only the whistling of the wind is to be heard again and the swinging of the door. The woman is silent, I am silent, I slowly drink my coffee, and if I seem to myself in those long minutes like a character from a film, it may be because I keep my hat on throughout this entire scene.

II

The Crab

1

I stayed in Cabo de Gata that night only because the old woman assured me that there was no afternoon bus back to Almería. I remember going all over the place—there wasn't a soul in sight—in search of a hotel or a boardinghouse. The words *ghost town* went through my head. Cats were straying around the expanses of wasteland to be seen everywhere. Almost all the bars were closed, and in the one I did find open a few of the locals were hunched in a dark corner, under hams hanging from the ceiling, and eyed me in silence as I asked the landlord where I could find accommodation.

La viuda, the landlord murmured, and he reluctantly pointed in the direction of the sea without looking at me, and although I did not understand the word (*La vida? La buda?*), it was clear to me that he meant the old woman in the restaurant on the promenade.

I remember something like pride of possession in her gestures and her voice as she showed me the flat-roofed annex on the north side of the restaurant, which faced away from the sea. She opened the first room on the right-hand wall of the corridor. It was level with the ground and just large enough to hold two beds, one on the left and one on the right, with space between them leading to a small but clean white-tiled bathroom. The old woman was asking two thousand pesetas a night, a figure that, divided by about eighty, gave you the equivalent in marks. I remember that late in the afternoon she made me a paella that cost as much as the room.

I remember the abrupt fall of darkness, and the yellow lights that all began to glow along the promenade at the same time.

I remember lying in my room and hearing a couple of leftover New Year fireworks going off.

I remember the cold, or more precisely I remember that my breath came out as vapor; I put on my pullover, crawled into my sleeping bag, and heaped all the spare blankets on top of me; I pushed my thermal mat between the edge of the bed and the wall, to ward off the cold radiating from it, although it would be more correct to say it was to protect me from the way the wall absorbed warmth.

So I lay in bed that evening, my numb fingers turning the pages of a book my friend Georg had given me for the journey. It was Henry Miller's *The Colossus of Maroussi,* in which the writer, who had just become internationally famous, described his visit to Greece—a whole succession of wonderful incidents; I remember mythical experiences while bathing in an isolated bay, driving through the mountains (were those vines growing on them?), incidents during which everyone was drunk, stoned, or incredibly happy in some other way.

The last straw was when I found that the hot water in my bathroom wasn't working. I fell asleep with the firm intention of going to Gibraltar next day, and on from Gibraltar to Africa.

I got up early in the morning and packed my things. I remember entertaining the idea (although it was only a fleeting thought) of going away without a word if I didn't happen to meet the landlady in the restaurant. But I did meet her.

The old woman seemed surprised to think of anyone wanting breakfast. I remember that she indicated to me, with a wealth of gestures, that she would go to the baker's to get some bread, and when I mentioned that I would like to catch the morning bus she claimed that today (it was Sunday) there was no morning bus, only a bus in the evening (which turned out to be correct—however, it also turned out that on other days there was a bus in the morning *and* the evening; in other words, the old woman had been lying to me the previous day).

She served me white bread with olive oil and a tomato for breakfast.

When I paid her for the night, I tried to get a price reduction because of the lack of hot water, but it was no use, although the old woman immediately went into the room with me and made it clear that she was inconsolable over that defect. At least I learned the word *fontanero,* which the old woman repeated several times with reference to the absence of hot water, a word I would probably never need again but all the same, as I knew at that moment, it was a word I would never in my life forget.

I asked the old woman if I could leave my rucksack in the restaurant, and I decided to go for a walk along the beach. The weather had changed, the sky was blue. I instinctively turned east, away from Almería and toward a small mountain range that fell steeply to the sea a few kilometers farther on. Of course I remember the brightly painted fishing boats drawn up on the sand just outside the little town, but when I think back to that walk it is not so much the boats that come to mind as the electric winches, or rather the ugly plastic or wooden housing that covered them, and the items standing around above the slope down to the beach, among the nets and fish crates—reminiscent in part of objets d'art, in part of tombstones—rusty engine parts, skeletal boats, old patches of oil, plastic bottles, and crumpled cigarette packs.

As I walked along I began picking up seashells automatically, without another thought, and I soon found myself throwing away the last shell when I found a more attractive one.

After some four or five kilometers, a church came into view on the road that ran parallel to the beach. It was obviously no longer in use, and when I looked at the small tower and the neo-Gothic ornamentation, honed by wind and weather to a shape I had never seen before, an idea that in my present circumstances was outlandish occurred to me: I thought the walls, once the Holy Ghost dwelling in them left, had simply *given up* resisting the laws of nature.

A little farther away lay a fenced tract of land with a mound of something white on it: salt, judging by appearances. Beyond this curious outpost lay a small village, its houses scattered among the agave plants as if at random. And beyond the village, as if it were the end of the world, rose a black mountain range.

On the way back something strange happened. The last and most beautiful shell I had picked up was a well-preserved little spiral conch. I had put it in the right-hand pocket of my jacket, and now, as I walked along lost in thought, I felt it. Suddenly my fingers encountered something hairy and wiry. Alarmed, I withdrew my hand from my pocket, and then carefully took out the shell. Two red feelers and two small pairs of pincers emerged from the shell itself; tiny, black button eyes seemed to be looking at me—the eyes of a hermit crab that had been living in my shell.

Although I thought poorly of astrology, and I could wax quite indignant when, for instance, my friend Georg showed that he was susceptible to such superstition, my find had a strange effect on me. It so happens that my star sign is Cancer. And now, searching for accommodation, I had found a crab in the home it had discovered for itself.

On the other hand, the crab was dead. It had obviously been washed up on the shore, and instead of leaving home it had stayed on until it dried up. Did that omen mean I should stay here or go?

I was now a few hundred meters from Cabo de Gata again. It was warm in the sun, there was still plenty of time before my bus left, so I took off my leather jacket and sat on it to look out to sea and toward Africa. Here I had another small encounter that led to a decision, although it is hard to say why.

A flock of small birds had come into my field of vision, probably seagulls of some kind. I had seen them earlier on my walk, and because of their behavior I called them *hysterical aunties,* on account of their curious habit of scuttling up and down the sloping shoreline, always avoiding the incoming waves. Stupid creatures, I thought—until I sat down on the beach and spent some time watching the birds.

In fact they were astonishing. They were not by any means running aimlessly about the beach; I soon realized they were pecking up plant remains of some kind from the damp slope, or microorganisms freshly washed ashore. They were small and had short legs, so they had no option but to keep running away from the waves lapping against the slope. But the precision with which they did it was surprising. I tried to estimate the range of a wave coming in. It is not by any means the tallest waves that always come in farthest. Apart from other factors (the inclination of the shore, the angle at which the wave approaches—how can anyone assess the "strength" of a wave within fractions of a second?), there are the additional complications of the water breaking against waves already streaming back, each of which in turn produces its own unpredictable swirls. It is, in short, *impossible* to calculate the range of any given wave. But the little birds can do it. They always run just ahead of the edge of the wave, no farther ahead than necessary but always far enough, and then they follow the water flowing back at the smallest possible distance, meanwhile performing this trick *as a flock,* all of them at once, in a single one hundred percent synchronized movement, which means, to be brief, that the birds at the upper edge of the group are not thinking just of themselves, but have to scurry far enough up the sloping shore to keep even the last birds, those at the lower edge, from getting their feathers wet.

I don't know how long I spent watching the hysterical aunties, perhaps an hour, perhaps only ten minutes. Anyway, I remember that after a while I stood up, that still in movement I whirled my leather jacket through the air as if to shake sand off it (which was not the point of my movement but the excuse for it)—and shouted out loud.

It was a brief shout. I don't know now what I shouted, whether it was a word or an obscenity. I don't think it was a word, I think it was simply a cry of rage, not of triumph, not a liberating roar, but a short sound of blatant annoyance that an outsider might have taken as my reaction to an insect bite.

2

I am very bad at haggling. I remember how, when Karolin and I
had separated and I was selling my Golf, a friendly young man of
Pharaonic appearance in a flowered shirt convinced me that by taking that heap of old scrap off my hands, even as a present, he would
be ruining himself; in the end I was even glad he gave me eight hundred marks for it—presumably about a quarter of what it was worth.

This time, however, was different. It was an odd negotiation between us: I the desperate stranger who hadn't mastered the Spanish
language, she the clever illiterate. I realized she was illiterate after she
refused, several times, to write down the sums about which we were
negotiating. *Mira, mira,* she kept saying, tapping herself briefly under
the eye, before she conveyed her offers to me in the manner and at the
speed of a deaf-mute, by holding up whole and half fingers. I lied for
all I was worth (just as she had lied to me about the times of bus de-
partures), telling her about lodgings in Almería that could be rented
for half the price. She flung her hands theatrically into the air, and
turned her tortoise-like head back and forth. I half-shouldered my
rucksack several times during our discussion, but on the other hand
I promised to stay for three months, and made out that I was still
undecided when we had finally fixed on the sum of twelve hundred
pesetas, including lunch.

I told her I was a writer (I had looked it up: *escritor*) and urgently
needed a table to write on (there wasn't one in my room), whereupon,
with the words *mesa, mesa,* she waved me over to the window, knock-
ing the big dining table with her knuckles as if she had to prove that
it was genuine, and finally she included a second cup of coffee at
breakfast in her offer. I hesitantly gave her my hand, and succeeded,

like the man in the flowered shirt when he bought my car, in making a face that suggested I had just sealed my fate.

The next day I bought:

- a brighter electric lightbulb
- six packs of candles, each containing twenty
- ten unlined A5 exercise books, along with a few pens that curiously enough turned out to write in purple ink

I bought the exercise books—of course—to write in, and if my grandchildren or great-grandchildren (supposing they are still reading books in their time) ask one day why I didn't have a laptop with me, I will say here, for the sake of clarity, that once there was a time when even prosperous people didn't have laptops, there was even a time *before* the laptop and *before* the cell phone, and although I write exclusively on a laptop now (and also have an iPhone on which I surreptitiously research my flight details while an actor reads my text aloud in Japanese or Finnish), that time was *my time,* and I am afraid I shall belong to it all my life, the way others identify themselves with a nation or a family.

I secretly screwed the electric lightbulb into the fitting of the dim 40-watt one, which I conscientiously put in my rucksack so that I could change them back again when I left.

I burned the candles—always six of them at once—in my room in the evening, thus raising the air temperature in the little place by some three or four degrees. I still couldn't do without the thermal mat, but at least my fingers were not clammy when I lay in bed in the evening and, having nothing else to do, read Henry Miller's *The Colossus of Maroussi.*

In the morning I took a cold shower, in spite of the slight bronchitis I had contracted, and in spite of the pitifully weak shower jet. I would probably have enjoyed bathing in the sea more, but I rejected that idea, no doubt because I was afraid the local inhabitants would think me crazy. Then I went to the baker's and bought myself a small *pan integral,* a kind of whole wheat baguette, entered the café, and sat down at my table. The old woman made me the coffee she had promised; I ate my *pan integral* with a little olive oil and a tomato (still green in parts) that she threw into the bargain. I warmed my hands on the hot coffee glass and wrote, my fingers still stiff with cold, the first sentence in one of the exercise books I had just bought.

That first sentence, if I remember correctly, was about small skewbald mongrels who all looked the same. What I do remember for certain is the bitter style I had developed overnight, so to speak (or over several nights), and the fierce rhythm in which my comprehensive disappointment found expression.

Later I sat on the bench outside the restaurant. The sun was high in the sky now and hot, but I recollect that I was still trembling with agitation inside. I dared not touch what I had written, I hardly even dared look at it. I simply sat there looking out to sea, on my knees the first exercise book, the blue one with the ring binding.

But at lunchtime my elation died down again. I was disturbed by the behavior of the young woman who served me that day (and on all the following days)—if you can call banging plates down without a word serving anyone. The big-bottomed girl, as I called her because of her truly gigantic behind, obviously belonged to the old woman's family, who all assembled around one of the tables at the back of the restaurant at lunchtime. I sat apart from them at my window table, and I remember that in view of the young woman's inexplicable hostility I was beginning to wonder whether I had done something wrong without knowing it. The food at least was reasonably good. There were three courses: salad, soup, and fish, and after the abrupt question *¿Blanco o tinto?*—the only words with which she favored me—the big-bottomed girl slammed a bottle of wine down on the table in front of me. At the end of the meal she gave me, in passing, an instant dessert in a plastic cup, which I ostentatiously ignored.

Then came the afternoon hours. Here I must admit that the afternoon is not my best time of day. As I am not really in any fit state to write then, I spend the afternoon in organizing my work, in the administration of my existence, an activity that now I am what people call successful has assumed monstrous proportions. But back then, in Cabo de Gata, there was no administration to be done, so all it amounted to was preserving myself from useless and generally deleterious attempts to go on writing. The hammock I had bought for my journey seemed to be just right for achieving embryonic passivity in my hours of leisure.

I remember setting out to find two suitable palms between which to sling my hammock. But on closer inspection, the palm trees growing in sparse groups around the town proved to be pitiful things, gray with flying sand and infested by small black insects. In spite of the sun a cold wind blew from the highlands, my back was freezing; and I remember that while I rocked myself in the hammock I couldn't rid myself of the idea that if I fell asleep, those little black beetles might crawl down my throat, and I even recollect mentally constructing insect-repellent devices, funnels made of cardboard through which I could run the strings of the hammock, always with the pointed ends of the funnels toward me, until I began to worry about the problem that the edges of the funnels would never stay the same distance from the strings passing through them, but would be brought down by their own weight, thus failing to achieve the desired effect.

I remember how, with the hammock under my arm and in an almost tearful mood, I stalked around Cabo de Gata, past the heaps of builders' rubble dusted with sand, and marveled at the small plots of land I found here and there in the desert; fenced-off sand! There were shabby wooden sheds on these plots, guarded by gigantic dogs baring their teeth.

I don't remember how I spent the evening.

But I do remember the next morning, in particular opening the shutters with my clammy fingers, looking up in timid expectation at the patch of sky above the alley—and finding it as spotlessly blue as the day before. I remember walking briskly, almost euphorically, to the baker's after my shower; I remember the old, black-clad saleswoman handing my *pan integral* over the counter as she had on the previous day with a nun-like expression, as if it was not a transaction but a blessing, so that I had no alternative to doing as I had the day before and putting my small amount of change into a charity box with a picture of Jesus, faded by the sun, stuck on it—and I recollect that these instances of déjà-vu gave me a sense of almost unholy joy; that on my way back I felt as if I had been walking along this beach promenade forever; that I even saw my ability to tell which way the wind was blowing from the weather vane as a sign that I felt at home.

3

I soon got used to moving to the bench outside the restaurant after breakfast, just before the sun rose above the crest of the low mountain range to the east. That was usually at about nine in the morning, and the timing was so reliable and predictable that before long I was moving out of doors two minutes in advance so as not to miss the moment of sunrise.

I remember the first glowing white dot shining above the black chain of mountains, swiftly growing until it was a mighty, dazzling disk, and I remember the immediate warmth and the pleasure, indeed, the sense of deliverance, it gave me. I had never before been so freezing cold as I was here in the south. And I had never before welcomed the sun with something like gratitude.

I remember the warm sense of well-being that gradually crept into my knees and the joints of my fingers; I remember my tense muscles beginning to relax until, very soon, a time came when I felt warm enough to take off my leather jacket, open my exercise book, and try to tune in to the grimly bitter tone that I needed to make any progress with my narrative.

I remember how the promenade, very slowly and gradually, began coming back to life; first came the dogs, the little Cabo pugs, as I lightheartedly called them, still arriving one by one at this early hour, suspiciously sniffing at the walls of the buildings and exploring every corner, as if the world had been created again overnight.

I remember the two men in striped pajamas who came out onto the promenade about a hundred meters farther east every morning; first one of them, who gazed at the sea for a long time with such an air of deliberate concentration that I wondered whether I had missed seeing something important out there. After a while a second man, also in pajamas, joined him. Usually the two of them stood together in silence, but now and then they embarked on a stormy argument. They would suddenly start shouting at each other, waving their arms about, advancing on one another with a menacing mien until one of them, after announcing some kind of final article of faith, swung theatrically around and marched away—only to turn and go back to his place silently and peacefully, as if nothing had happened.

I remember the women who came to help in the kitchen (including the big-bottomed girl), or to be precise I remember the clamor that came from the kitchen once they had arrived; the women shouted at one another too, and it was some time before I realized that there was no hostility in the noise they made, and fundamentally it wasn't even shouting at all, simply an intonation that, like the missing *s* sound at the ends of words, was part of the Andalusian dialect.

I remember that for a long time I wrote nothing, but gazed out to sea; that I suddenly had a strong sense of belonging to all this, or conversely that all this was part of my story, even the dogs, who, to be honest, no longer all looked the same to me. I remember how I tore the pages I had written out of my blue exercise book and wrote a different, less bitter first sentence in what was now a new, empty one.

But then midday comes. I remember the face (white as porcelain in spite of the southern sun) of the young woman who serves me my lunch without ever changing her expression. I remember her turning her behind to me after she slams my plate down and moving toward the family's table, her buttocks, each the size of half a pumpkin, wobbling alternately. And sitting at my special table, I feel more excluded than ever.

I try to make out whether they are talking about me at their family table, whether, when they laugh, they are laughing at me; and the discovery that they are not eating the same salad as mine, are drinking a different wine, or having chicken instead of the fish served to me every day, is enough to make me feel I am at a disadvantage.

Then I lie in the hammock again; I have put my thermal mat in it to protect myself from the chilly wind, but there is no protection from the thoughts going through my head. I get out of the hammock and once again try going for walks over the desert, where garbage lies all over the place.

Once I find a suitcase, an aluminum flight case, quite new, locked and with a name on it; curiously, I even think I still know the name (Andreas Hetzel). For a moment I wonder whether I ought to tell the police about it, but the idea that they might want to know my place of residence or ask for confirmation of my identity keeps me from doing so—and the next day the case has disappeared.

Once I find a dead cat, a ginger tabby, what's left of it. Its body is so badly burned that the backbone is exposed; its mouth is open wide as if in a scream.

And once, when I walk all the way around Cabo de Gata, I come upon a large, shallow lake with pink flamingos stalking about in it. In fact, these flamingos, as I then discover in my travel guide, are among the main attractions of the place. There is even a small blind, where you can look through a slit in the wooden wall and watch the birds standing on one leg for hours on end (a skill that strikes me as admirable, yes, but deadly boring).

Later I sit on my bench again and watch the sun sinking into the sea in the evening, large and red and round, as predictably as it rises above the mountains in the morning. The lights along the promenade flicker on. It gets cold. I go to my room and light candles. I sit on the edge of the bed, eating a little of the manchego cheese that I have bought myself and drinking the cheap local red wine with it, until at last I go to bed and, for want of anything else to do, pick up Miller's book again.

In fact, it was the only book I had brought, so as to save on weight. So steadily, if with some hesitation, I make my way through *The Colossus of Maroussi,* and although, as I said before, I hardly remember anything about the book itself (and I stick to my principle of not taking it off the shelf where it stands today with many of its pages dog-eared, marking my disagreements with the author), I remember very well my increasing annoyance with its spiritual or, as I thought, esoteric presumption. I remember letting the book sink on my chest again and again, and thinking of my friend Georg (who had recommended it for my journey as the best thing Miller ever wrote). I remember our arguments about anything and everything—the transmigration of souls, morphogenetic fields—and in particular I remember how once, after we had cut up a cod we had just caught, sprinkled it with lemon, and watched the fillets twitching although they had already been taken off the bone, we argued fiercely over the question of whether there were people whose mere presence could influence the life span of electrical appliances—a difference of opinion that had led to the only serious disagreement between us to date.

But then, the next morning, I am sitting on my bench again, the first glimmer of sunlight shows above the black mountains, shines more brightly, spreads, sends its life-giving heat out into the world, and in view of that sun, skeptical as I am, it seems to me entirely absurd, positively deranged, to doubt the existence of God.

4

I may have spent two weeks, no more but not much less, writing opening sentences in the morning on pages that I tore out in the afternoon; anyway, this went on so long that, as I still remember, I had used all the paper in my blue ring-bound exercise book and had just begun writing in the green one when the Englishman arrived.

I remember the backfiring noise of the huge motorbike, gleaming with chrome, that was coming toward me from the other end of the beach promenade. A figure clad in black leather dismounted, his head in a motorbike helmet like an astronaut's, beneath which a run-of-the-mill, almost childlike face came into view, indeed what might be described as the face from a casting call, and the young man whose face it was asked me where you could spend the night here.

I remember being rather put out when the man—I've forgotten his name—sat down on the bench beside me without more ado and, although it was obvious I was busy with something else, began telling me, unasked, where he had come from (I think it was Granada) and where he planned to go next (I think it was Málaga); however, I asked politely where his home was and was surprised to hear him say England. I had immediately assumed he was American because of his crass behavior (or perhaps because he reminded me of the film *Easy Rider*).

I remember that we ate together. The big-bottomed young woman served us, but oddly enough her manner was less chilly than usual when the Englishman joined me at my table. He actually managed to get her to speak, although his Spanish was even worse than mine. And when she turned away from us, her pumpkin-like buttocks wobbling, the Englishman rolled his eyes and made a barely audible sound, clicking his rolled-up tongue a couple of times suggestively, putting me off yet making me wonder whether that incredibly fat but taut, jutting bottom, always presented in skintight and often bright red pants by the woman, who otherwise was not unattractive nor even fat—making me wonder, as I say, whether that rear end might hold any erotic attraction for me, in defiance of my more northern ideas of the physical ideal.

I remember that after lunch the Englishman was bent on going to look at the flamingos. I remember the large camera with which, constantly pressing the shutter release, he approached the banks of the flamingos' lake. I remember my annoyance at the way he ignored all the notices forbidding tourists to do this or that, put up to protect the birds. But I also remember that to my surprise—for I hadn't known they could fly—the birds stalking along the bank suddenly rose into the air in a beautiful pink formation.

After that we played billiards. Although the Englishman had only just arrived he knew that in the center of Cabo de Gata, right beside the palm-fringed square, there was a bar with a billiards table. It was an ordinary little bar, the kind of place where people throw parties, with a television set hung under the ceiling and running nonstop, and a weedy pockmarked bartender who wore a gold chain around his neck.

We were the only guests. After the Englishman had beaten me twice with humiliating ease, he gave me a lesson, explaining how to hold the cue and move your fingers on it; how to play the balls and make the white ball stop after it has been hit, or alternatively how to make it run on or turn right or left. After that I still always lost, but at least I managed to sink a ball in the pocket now and then.

Later we sat on the bench and had a few cans of beer. I remember the vast starry sky above us. I can still feel the wind on my face as the Englishman told me his story. To my surprise, he was a miner, and in fact I now noticed his large hands, which, it seemed, found it hard to hold a can of beer without squeezing it out of shape.

His story was as follows: a few years ago he had married, and with his wife bought a small row house in a dilapidated condition, if I understood him properly, which he was going to remodel himself. But almost as soon as they had bought the house his wife divorced him. After that, he told me, he hadn't gone to work anymore, he hadn't gone out at all. He had spent a year alone in his house, staring at the walls. Then, only a few weeks ago, he had sold the house, bought the motorbike with the proceeds, and set off on his travels.

He asked how long I had been here.

About a month, I told him.

Then he wanted to know what I did with myself all day here, and I remember the little dialogue that followed almost verbatim.

I'm trying to write a book, I said in English.

Wow, great, said the Englishman in the same language. What about? That's not clear yet, I said.

Hmm, said the Englishman, and he nodded, or rather he rocked back and forth, leaning forward from the waist. He rocked until his rocking no longer had anything to do with my answer. Until it was clear he wasn't going to ask any more questions about it, whether out of consideration or lack of interest. And partly because after he had told me his own story I didn't want to seem unforthcoming, partly because I didn't want to make a fool of myself, I told him the story of the suitcase.

Or more precisely, the story of the man who, in the middle of a deep personal crisis, broke, divorced, unsuccessful, travels to Cabo de Gata and finds a flight case in the wasteland outside it.

The story began with the detail, which was far from the facts, that because the man is a chemist by training he destroys the lock of the case with the aid of a cleaning fluid containing sodium chloride (which would work only—and only theoretically—with aluminum, although as a rule such locks are made of steel on which chemicals have no effect). But the Englishman accepted it, and I went on with my story in halting English.

I don't remember the words now, only the images: the carefully packed clothes in the case (which happen to be the right size for the man in my story). And the image of the German passport that he finds (and that I now see in my mind's eye as red, although I think German passports were green at the time). He also finds a fax from Paris confirming a reservation in a luxury hotel.

I also remember another detail: the man in my story, using the pen with purple ink that he has bought in the little Cabo de Gata supermarket, manages to forge the official stamp on the corner of his photograph and sticks it in the stranger's passport, before putting on the clothes he has found and going to Paris with his new identity.

Now that's interesting, said the Englishman.

And at that moment my interest in the story was extinguished. I no longer wanted to make up what happened next; indeed, I even remember disliking the Englishman's sudden reaction.

I haven't thought it out any further, I said.

And I was also annoyed by the way the Englishman praised me as you might praise a schoolboy.

But it's exciting, he said. It will be a huge success. You must go on with it. And so on, and so forth.

Then he asked me to tell him my full name so that, he said, he could look for the book when it was published. And as I had already told him my first name, I said:

Handke. Peter Handke.

We said no more after that—or did we? Did he talk about the sea, or the moon, or my story? All I know is that the constellation of Orion stood in the sky, and I marveled at it. And that I asked myself where my fatal, ruinous, irrational wish to write came from. I remember the sudden amazement and even anger rising in me. I thought of my many failed attempts and all the torments I inflicted on myself. It was, I thought, obviously idiotic to spend my life like this, in an old-fashioned, self-destructive activity, one that didn't even make me any money! I knew all about that. I had done a good deal of research into the background of that woman who wrote the biographies of cats and dogs. Even if I finished a novel, even if that novel was printed by a large and highly regarded publishing house, it would be stupidity and self-deception to expect to sell much more than a print run of three thousand copies, or, to put it in numbers, that I would earn more than nine thousand marks from work on which I had squandered months or more likely years of my life, giving up my apartment and my medical insurance for its sake, work that had wrecked my personal relationships and that my father would never consider anything but one of my quirks.

Let's go, said the Englishman.

I remember how he squeezed the beer can in his large miner's paw. I remember the sound of the metal crushing. And I remember that when we said good night, I made up my mind to ask him in the morning whether I could hitch a ride on his motorbike and leave Cabo de Gata with him.

5

After two days the Englishman thinks he has seen everything there is to see in Cabo de Gata, and goes on toward Gibraltar. I stay behind and return to my usual daily routine. Although with minor alterations.

I've taken to playing billiards. I always play in the afternoon, when I come back to the village after my excursions. I have become used to walking on the beach every day, or more precisely on the way there—the way where?—I walk along the beach; on the way back I go a few hundred meters inland and walk along the banks of the flamingo lakes, from which also, it turns out, salt is harvested. They are artificial basins in which seawater gradually evaporates, leaving behind, as you can see in some of them, a dead, dirty crust of salt.

At the same time every day I go into the bar, where the weedy bartender sits behind the counter blindly polishing glasses while he looks up at his TV set.

If I were at liberty to invent a different temperament for the bartender I probably would, simply to introduce some variety into my characters. But as I have decided to write only what I remember, I have no choice but to describe him as stoic and taciturn, like the big-bottomed woman—with the difference that our little daily ritual is beginning to interest and even amuse me. It goes like this:

I wish him good day. He doesn't return the compliment. Instead, he goes on looking at his TV set for a while before turning to me—none too soon!—lifting his chin to show that he is ready to take my order.

I order coffee. I order coffee every day. All the same, he lifts his chin in a silent query every day. Every day he goes over to his machine, and once he has taken his attention away from the TV set, he devotes it to the machine for some time, then places a cookie in a heat-sealed wrapping and a little tube of sugar on the saucer of my cup of coffee, although I ostentatiously leave them on the counter every day, and the only part of the little drama that has changed in the course of time is that, since my hundred pesetas are lying ready for him on the counter, he can save himself the single word, *¡Cien!* that he used to utter.

Then I drink my coffee and we both look up at the TV set, where a Spanish soap opera is always running. I remember some of its characters: cool black people in convertibles, painfully beautiful women moving their hips as if they were in urgent need of sexual satisfaction; pale buff-colored catacombs with wild young men in them clutching microphones and standing in unnatural attitudes, or smashing guitars as if no one had ever smashed a guitar before.

After finishing my coffee, I put a coin in the slot of the billiards table and play a round of billiards against myself, the solids against the stripes. However the game turns out, I always feel that I have lost.

Meanwhile—as if to prove that failing to return a greeting is not an Andalusian custom—after a month the men who come to the promenade restaurant for their midday meal at the large family table every day do begin to acknowledge my presence, at first silently, from the doorway, as they come in and see me sitting at my table.

One day, after the meal, the old woman sits down with me to ask if everything is all right, and I take this chance to complain about the instant dessert; from then on I get a delicious orange instead, fragrantly flavored with vanilla. I realized long ago that the old woman is the boss here. She negotiates with workmen, orders what she needs, and works out quantities for her suppliers on her fingers; the suppliers, frowning, then check her arithmetic on their pocket calculators. *Todo mio,* she tells me as we sit at my table together, in a portentous tone of voice that suggests the cackling of chickens in the way it rises from the depths: *It's all mine.* Her husband, she tells me, is dead. I don't entirely understand what he died of, but I recollect the half-reassuring, half-dismissive gesture letting me know, when I try to look sympathetic, that it was all a long time ago—too long ago.

I also learn that the three men who have taken to acknowledging me are her sons. All three are fishermen, all three have their own boats—photographs hang on the wall showing them in front of these boats, generally holding up fish of an impressive size. I sometimes meet one of the sons on my walks, when I pass the moorings on the outskirts of the village. His name is Alfredo; he is the eldest of the three brothers, owns the largest boat, a cutter really, and is always tinkering with it. Once, as I pass, he calls to me as he disentangles separate fish from the mesh of his net. *¡Mucho trabajo, poco pescado!* A lot of work, not many fish! After that I call, every time I see him on the beach beside his boat: *¡Mucho trabajo!* And every time he replies: *¡Poco pescado!* And I am moved almost to tears by this little play on words. It could hardly be put more concisely and it links the two of us, strangers as we are to each other, in close complicity.

In fact, the fishermen's catch is pitifully small, and seems to bear no relation to the effort of bringing it in. Even hauling the boats up on the beach is laborious. The larger fishing boats in particular are difficult to move over the sand. Heavy planks with ropes around them are placed under the keel, and while the cable of the engine's winch is stretched taut enough to hum, they have to be pulled away behind the boat and inserted in front of it, until it reaches the desired berth. As I watch, I feel a little ashamed of myself for my disappointment, as a tourist, when I found out that the boats here were drawn up on shore mechanically these days and not by hand.

But then I see the fishermen tipping black oil into the sand, dropping empty plastic bottles anywhere and everywhere, and I smell the diesel of the boats' engines, blown for hundreds of meters by the wind. On my walks, I see the large quantities of garbage washed up by the sea every day, and it seems to me right and even proper that this ravaged, poisoned, exploited sea produces hardly any fish at all today, and maybe a time will come when it produces none.

I still watch the sunset daily (it comes about a minute later every day).

I still light candles in the evening, eat manchego cheese and drink red wine with it.

I have finished reading Miller's novel. I now read *El País* instead, although it is always the same edition. Many years ago my grandmother told me how she taught herself Spanish in her Mexican exile by reading the same newspaper again and again before going to sleep until, she said, she understood the text. I am trying the same method. I read the article about the introduction of the European internal market—the *mercado interior*—over and over again, and understand nothing about it. Or is there really an EU norm for the smallest size of onions? I try to imagine a committee of serious men sitting somewhere in a distant office building, negotiating the correct diameter of onions and strawberries . . . an odd image.

I do more or less understand a report saying that legal proceedings against Erich Honecker have been suspended.

I also understand (now that I come to think of it, I wonder whether it wasn't a misunderstanding, but I do remember that even then I wondered about it) that fishermen were now among the professional groups with the highest rate of lung cancer, and I looked up the vocabulary several times in my little yellow dictionary, to make sure.

I remember a dream I had at this time, and because I remember it I will write it down here. It took place in my parents' former apartment, a huge one with five rooms, but I was in the smallest of them, a little place behind the kitchen smelling of photographic fixing salt and shoe cream. I had invited my editor from the radio station to this little room, where you could hardly sit down, for a meal, and I recollect working in the kitchen with my pots and pans as I told the radio editor, who was sitting in the tiny room, the story of my mother's death—as if I were trying to *sell* it to him. I remember that the memory of my mother affected me more strongly than it ever did in waking life; I remember the pain in my throat; I remember how I tried to cover up my grief, while the rather distracted radio editor, who was obviously in a bad mood, tried fitting his knees around the old bedside table placed in this little room to hold shoe-cleaning materials. I was awoken—in the middle of the night—by the pain in my throat.

But then it is morning again. I inspect the sky. The sky is blue. I go to the baker's, and it strikes even me as crazy, while I look with pleasure for the weather vane, that I am in such a good mood every morning, day after day, although I haven't yet written a single line.

I sit on my bench. The dogs arrive, first one—always the same one, the one I like least (in the morning, when he is on his own, he doesn't venture to pass my bench but slinks down to the beach behind the little balustrade). Then come the pajama-clad men with their argument. And then—the most remarkable novelty that day—comes the woman with her leg in a plaster walking cast.

She approaches from the other end of the promenade. One day she appears there, limps all along the promenade with her plaster cast, comes toward me and then passes me, turning down one of the last alleys off the promenade. And all the way the woman is wailing, complaining—obviously about the hardship she has to bear: a monotonous singsong under her breath that seems to be directed at me, because there is no one else to be seen on the promenade. The woman is as round as a globe, she has curly hair that sticks out curiously, she rocks in time to her limping steps like a roly-poly toy—all the same, only after several days of the same performance do I realize who this woman reminds me of: our civics teacher at school, Fräulein Kubick.

Fräulein Kubick rocked her rounded body back and forth just like that, although she didn't wear a plaster walking cast. Her curly hair stood out from her head in just the same way. She chanted in just the same soporific tone of complaint as she walked—slowly, slowly—between our rows of desks, announcing the basic laws of the dialectical method—making the pauses between the words long enough for you to fall asleep—as she asked the *fundamental philosophical question* for the hundredth time, a question that, because it had already been asked a hundred times, no one was prepared to repeat. No answer was required, because in a socialist educational institution it was so obvious that even Fräulein Kubick would never have thought that anyone could offer a deviant reply. No, she wanted to hear the question, that would have been enough, and the fact that no one came up with it was always a severe disappointment to her, obliging her to ask the fundamental philosophical question again herself, for the last time: namely, the question that divided philosophers into materialists and idealists:

Can. Pause. The world. Pause. Be. Pause. Perceived?

And wasn't she right, I think, as the imitation Fräulein Kubick totters past me, isn't that *really* the fundamental question?

Then the American arrived.

6

Of course the American looked exactly as I imagined an Englishman: pants with neat creases and cuffs, a green waxed jacket, a face like a horse's—forgive me this silly prejudice—and thin, reddish hair that from time to time, and obviously unsuccessfully, was combed back from a parting.

He stood there beside my bench, a man distinctly too tall for this part of the world, carefully apologizing for disturbing me before he asked where one could spend the night here.

I saw him again at lunch, when he sat down at my table, again with a civil request for permission first. He tried to order in Spanish, with a rubbery accent but trying to be grammatically correct in an almost ridiculous way. I must admit I was relieved when the big-bottomed girl ended it, or so I felt anyway under the spell of her proximity, with a sharp *¿Blanco o tinto?* Only after she had rolled away, turning her mighty buttocks to us, did I see the red flush come into the American's face, and I remember making an apologetic face because I had watched those alternately wobbling pumpkin halves with such unconcealed interest.

We went for a walk together that afternoon, a longer walk than any of my previous expeditions. We passed the place with the church that the Holy Ghost had left, and the huge mounds of salt, and then climbed the range of low mountains behind which the sun rose in the morning. Somewhere up there a lighthouse stood, although I hardly remember it now. I do clearly recollect, however, the view from the winding road down over the wide bay and the village of Cabo de Gata, pale in the afternoon sun so that you could hardly distinguish it from its surroundings, like something washed up by the sea. And like something that sooner or later would be washed away again.

On the climb down, I think, the American told me he had just arrived from Saudi Arabia, where he had been working for two or three years as a teacher of English. Now he was on vacation and wanted to see Europe, or at least the south of Europe: Spain, Italy, and France. He said very little about Saudi Arabia, as if it was hardly worth mentioning. But I do remember what he said about the women there, or not so much what he said as how he said it, and he wasn't really talking about the Saudi Arabian women at all but about their absence. I remember how he hesitated, and stopped, his hands grasping thin air as he tried to explain what it meant not to hear a woman's voice or touch a woman's hand for months on end, to see nothing but the occasional glint of a pair of eyes behind a burka. And I remember the red flush on his cheeks when he told me that a woman's proximity—quite independently of her appearance and her age—always confused him.

From that moment on, he struck me as a desperate man. Everything about him seemed to express that desperation: his limp gestures, his silence when he was silent, his American accent when he spoke, his laughter when, later, he sank the black ball into the pocket by mistake while we were playing billiards. And when I let him win after he had lost to me three or four times, he sighed as if after a defeat and nodded, with his lips closed over his teeth, like a man stifling pain.

Then we bought two overpriced bottles of red wine from the weedy bartender, asked him for paper cups, and went out on the beach promenade. The wind was blowing harder, a positively stormy wind, surprisingly warm, coming from Africa. The American was full of enthusiasm. He didn't want to sit on the bench outside the restaurant; he insisted on finding a place on the nocturnal beach—and I was drunk enough by then to go along with him.

So we sat in the sand, stared into the darkness where the sea was roaring like a huge animal on a chain, and I remember being sud-

denly reminded of those mythical monsters who were thrown down
to the underworld by Uranus, the father of the Greek gods.

The American asked me what I was doing here in Cabo de Gata. I
remember saying that I didn't really know. And I remember his disappointment. When he saw me sitting on that bench early in the morning, he said, he had thought I was a writer.

Later, when we had finished most of our supply of wine, he con-
fessed that he himself wanted to write, and had really gone to that
goddamned Saudi Arabia to finance his novel.

I asked what it was about.

That's a difficult question, said the American.

I asked what the plot of the novel was (I think I used the word
story), and suddenly we were in the middle of a conversation about
literature, in particular European and American literature. It turned
out that the American not only thought highly of European literature but knew far more about it than I did.

I remember he talked about Flaubert, whom he regarded as the
first of all modern novelists; he loved the great Russians (which did
not surprise me at all); had read the whole of *Ulysses* (unlike me); he
admired Arno Schmidt and even Uwe Johnson, while on the whole
he suspected American literature of triviality.

He could just about accept my admiration of William Faulkner.
He thought Updike, so far as I recollect, too slight. When I cited
Paul Auster in defense of contemporary American literature, he
hadn't read him at all. And although he had nothing to say against
Nabokov, he refused to count him as an American writer.

Americans, he shouted against the stormy wind, think literature
is all about the plot! I remember his scornful laughter. I remember
how he interrupted himself in pouring his wine, throwing up his
arms with the bottle of red in his right hand and the paper cup in
his left. And I remember how his reddish hair, still catching enough
light from above the shadow of the balustrade, blazed on his head.

Then he emptied his cup, stood up, tottered down to the sea, and suddenly began playing the game of the hysterical aunties. I remember him feeling his way after the ebbing wave with his big feet, going as far as he could over the seabed as it was revealed. Trying to get away from the next wave coming in. He almost managed it twice. The wave got him on the third attempt. I see him climbing out of the sea, shoes dripping, pants wet to just below the knee. He laughs, he calls out something, beats his wings. But what I see is the hundred-armed creatures reaching out for him, the monsters cast down into the underworld by Uranus.

7

There are seven puzzles in Cabo de Gata.

The first is the puzzle of the dog shit, or rather its absence. Considering all the dogs around the place, why, I asked myself from my first day in Cabo de Gata on, is there never any dog shit on the promenade?

The second is the puzzle of the plots of land in the desert with dilapidated huts on them, guarded by black shepherd dogs. What, I wondered, are they for? They aren't community gardens suitable for rest and recreation. Do people bring valuable objects of some kind here on purpose, to have them guarded by dogs baring their fangs?

The third puzzle is that suitcase. Why would someone leave his case in the desert? Quite a new wheeled suitcase, a item of some value in itself. The mere idea of anyone pulling a suitcase like that through the sandy desert is absurd. And above all, I tell myself, wouldn't I have been bound to see the owner of the case in this flat landscape?

The fourth puzzle is the green tomatoes that turned up on the beach one day. You may wonder what's so odd about that. A ship has lost a few crates of tomatoes, maybe they slipped overboard in a storm . . . but as soon as I start thinking about it the matter gets mysterious, and the more I think about it the more mysterious it is: since when have tomatoes been transported on the deck of a ship in bright sunlight? And how can the tomatoes all have come ashore at once, covering a space about the size of a European handball court with hardly a gap between them? Also, how did they manage, days after the last storm, to get to the top of the sloping beach?

I am not quite sure whether I include the hysterical aunties as I count up the puzzles, but the tower is certainly another of them.

I ought to have written about the tower long before, because I see it every day; I pass it every day, although only recently—since the American left—have I realized what a puzzle it is: a mighty building, standing high above all the houses of Cabo de Gata. It is round and thick and loamy yellow. It looks like a chess piece. Like the tower of a fortress, but without the fortress. Instead it is surrounded by a wall only one brick thick, and a little taller than a man. It appears relatively paltry; you feel you could easily kick it down. And there is another detail that in a clumsy, almost childish way tries to lend the tower the character of a fortress: the entrance door is three or four meters above ground level, and a steep flight of steps rises, a construction on its own, in front of this door, stopping a meter away from the tower high above it, with a small drawbridge crossing the gap between them. Above the entrance, as if stuck in place by a proud householder with his own hands, are shiny navy blue tiles with white letters on them, evidently explaining the purpose of the building: *Guardia Civil.*

But what exactly does that explain? Why does a village like Cabo de Gata need such a building? Even stranger, why does this building stand so close to the beach, in the sand of the shore, right beside the fishing boats? It isn't a police station (the Cabo de Gata police station is in a small building in the center of the village); it is too massive and squat for an observation tower, built for strength rather than height. On the other hand, it isn't fit to be a fortress, and would stand up only to medieval weapons at the most. A bulwark against pirates? Against attacking Moors? Except that it would never be able to defend the village, or anything but perhaps itself. A building constructed for its own defense?

That's the sixth puzzle. The seventh is the coffin.

It has been lying there since the night of the storm, since the night when the American disappeared. At least, I last saw him that night, and the last thing I remember is how he was trying to imitate the hysterical aunties flapping their wings. It lies roughly there, maybe a little farther out toward the sea or maybe not (for I have no idea just how far we went that night when we were drunk)—almost exactly between Cabo de Gata and the salt village.

A sea coffin, what else? A plain, already rather weather-beaten metal container, big enough to take a human being, even a very tall one. The storm didn't manage to wash it right up on dry land, so it lies stranded between land and water. The waves lap around the thing, gurgling.

Of course my reason tells me that it can't be a coffin. Would the authorities simply leave a coffin lying on the shore? But perhaps no one has noticed it yet? Or maybe because the coffin straddles two districts, the authorities are discussing which of them is responsible for it? Or maybe they think some authority to do with the sea ought to be salvaging it?

I make a pilgrimage every afternoon to see if it is still there. My walks suddenly have a purpose, a destination. They are all the same—apart from those small changes that the sea makes daily, washing up flotsam, carrying it away; apart from the sounds that change every day; apart from the constantly changing color of the water, which varies between silver gray and turquoise blue, depending on the strength of its movement.

I have stopped collecting shells now that I have found some really beautiful ones, a shell for each woman in my life. A prickly spiral shell, pink inside, for Karolin. And although of course Sarah is not one of my women, isn't even a woman at all yet, I have dedicated a shell to her: a white, smooth Venus clam shell that lies on the narrow windowsill of my room along with the others. It is rather shamefully like the part of a woman that its name refers to, and when I pick it up and touch its gentle undulations I feel a little criminal.

Instead I look for hag stones: stones with a hole through them. Flints won't do. Beside the Baltic, I remember, Karolin and I once seriously debated the question of whether flints with holes in them were genuine hag stones. Here, in Cabo de Gata, there are few flints, and the idea that something—although what?—depends on the kind of stone I find weighs on my mind. I don't venture to think about it too hard. If I find a beautiful round stone, then it is beautiful and round; if I find a small flat stone, then it's small and flat; and if I let a flint qualify, then it is deceitful, because that's deception.

Incidentally, I have already found a hag stone twice. The first was very unsymmetrical, with its hole very close to the edge, and the other one looked like a growth. I threw both away, literally; I threw them into the sea. Now I have to find another, I must, because if I don't, if I don't . . .

So I walk along, looking down, searching the ground. Crushed shells crunch beneath my feet. Here and there I see small patches of pebbles. I mustn't stand still—that's a strange rule. Walking slowly is allowed. I stride on, the pebbles crunch. Above me the gulls cry their alarm. I hear them but do not see them. I search and search . . . because if I don't find a hag stone, then . . . then what? The sea chuckles. It chatters. The sea breathes. The sea is suddenly still for a moment and then another moment . . . only the wind plays organ music in my ears—and then the sound of the sea is back. Speaking with a splutter of laughter, as if it had played a trick on me.

Then I reach the casket. I turn around to face Africa. I straighten up, looking ahead of me. Now the wind is blowing in my face. Suddenly I am humming the tune of "The Star-Spangled Banner." Jimi Hendrix taught it to me in his famous appearance at Woodstock: people said Jimi Hendrix was tearing the American national anthem to shreds, but anyway what was left of it was enough to imprint the tune on my mind forever, the rich triad at the beginning that falls on its feet, D major if I'm not mistaken, and then the sound rises up and up in the air, the heroic tone of the Fender Stratocaster guitar as Hendrix played it is what I hear when I hum the tune of the American national anthem half to myself, yet at the same time over the wide expanse of the sea. With my hand to the brim of my hat, in a military salute, I stand there observing the last rites for my fallen American friend.

On the way back I go into the bar with the billiards table. I sit at the counter sipping the coffee that the bartender still serves me with sugar and a cookie. I stare at the TV set: a peephole into another world. And wonder whether *that* world may not be the real one, and the world in which I am sitting an illusion?

Suddenly the sunset strikes me as artificial. I sit on my bench, trying to feel that I am on Planet Earth, that I am moving through space, turning backward—but what I see is a red disk being slowly pulled down into the sea, as if by an invisible string.

Then I go to my room, read the Spanish newspaper for the umpteenth time: reports of EU commissioners arguing about the diameter of onions and strawberries; from the head of a forgotten state.

Eating manchego cheese helps a little. Why do things taste best in their places of origin? Even though nothing material is lost in transport, or at least that can't be proved.

Then I light my six candles, and lie down on the bed. I stare at the six shadows that begin to quiver slightly after a while, the flames hopping. And after a while I myself begin to quiver and shake.

That, if I remember correctly, was the evening before the evening when the cat appeared.

III

The Cat

1

Some time ago I had written several postcards: I felt duty bound to let my father know, at long last, where I was; I wrote Georg a card saying that the streetlights here were powered by the mental energy of swarms of flying fish; and for Sarah, because I had promised her I would write, I had chosen a picture postcard with a touch of Africa about it, and I told her about flamingos and palm trees and said the sun shone every day here—something I hoped Karolin (who would presumably read the postcard too) would envy me.

Then the postcards lay around for a while on the floor of my room because I had no stamps, and the little post office was always closed when I passed it. And then, when I finally bought stamps, I threw away the card half-written with Karolin in mind for that very reason, even though I had already stuck a stamp on it, and decided to write Sarah another one.

It was yet another few days before I had a postcard and in particular a stamp for it, and then at last I wrote Sarah the card one evening—about Three-Gram-Kvowch, the little creature that was accidentally thrown away in the garbage but had been resurrected here in the desert in order to play a game of Yackety-Yak with me every day; I promised to explain the rules of Yackety-Yak to Sarah when I was back again.

It was around eight in the evening when I set off again for the mailbox, which was less than a hundred meters away, close to the promenade, and on the side street along which the woman with the plaster cast on her leg used to disappear. I was glad that I had finally written the card, and was humming cheerfully to myself. But I also remember that as the card vanished into the mailbox I was overcome by sadness; the idea of Sarah holding that card was suddenly very close, taking me back for several seconds to the apartment where we had lived together for nearly ten years. I could almost smell the raffia mats in the corridor (I was the only one who cleaned them from time to time), I saw the worn-out slatted roller blind in front of the bookshelves at the end of the corridor (Karolin always pulled it up untidily), I remembered the cistern I had provisionally repaired years ago . . . and thinking of all that I almost missed hearing the quiet mew behind me.

I turned around, and there she was: a ginger tabby like the charred dead cat I had found out in the desert. I crouched down and spoke to her. She mewed but did not come closer. I turned to walk away, and the cat followed me.

She kept the same distance of about two or three meters between us all the time. When I stopped, she stopped too. If I walked back toward her she retreated. But if I walked on again, going the same way as before, she went on following me. Clever, I thought. A clever, cautious creature. In a place where people strike cats dead, or (who knows?) pour gasoline over them and set them on fire, distrust is only too well justified.

But why was she following me? Why made her think that I, of all people, would give her something? Had she learned to expect good things from people who went to the mailbox? Had she learned that such people were not usually local inhabitants—not the kind who set fire to cats? Was she confusing me with someone else? Was it my scent, if she could pick it up? Was it my voice? (I had been humming "The Star-Spangled Banner" on my way.) Or were people who went to the mailbox typically in a mood favorable to cats?

Anyway, she followed me the full hundred meters back. It seemed to me a long way. I stopped again several times to repeat the experiment, always with the same result: she stopped as well, always just outside the range of any potential kick, but as soon as I began to move she followed. Now I wanted to find out how far we could take this game.

I went back to the restaurant annex where I was staying. She followed me. First I opened the door to the corridor on the ground floor, then the door of my room, around the corner to the right. I left both doors open. Took the glass ashtray off the windowsill and put a few crumbs of my expensive manchego cheese in it. Put it down just inside the room, close to the door. Sat on my bed and waited.

Sure enough, the cat followed. She appeared in the doorway, as silent as a ghost, looked carefully around to make sure there was a way of escape. Then she ate the pieces of manchego cheese from the ashtray.

Her tail, stretched out just above the floor, was quivering.

Now and then a soft rasping sound, like the growl of a beast of prey, emerged from her jaws. When she had finished, she licked her mouth, showing her tiny pink tongue, narrow but astonishingly long, like those chocolate cats' tongues I remembered from my childhood.

When I cautiously stood up she ran away.

I remember that next day—just in case—I put two small shrink-wrapped sausages, already reduced in price, in my supermarket basket. I felt a little embarrassed about getting them past the checkout, but the young checkout girl with blond streaks in her hair looked at me as usual, that's to say in the way young checkout girls with blond streaks in their hair do look at a man of forty—a man in a leather jacket, a checked shirt, and a felt hat faded by the sunlight.

About eight in the evening I went to the mailbox again, although I had nothing to post this time. And yes, there was the cat! Once again she followed me at a carefully calculated distance. Once again

I opened the two doors and put the ashtray with food in it down for her. But before doing so I tapped the blade of my Opinel knife on the glass rim of the ashtray, so that she would remember the ringing sound, and it would convey a message to her.

The next day I bought cat food: a blue can with a young, blue-eyed cat on the label. For the first time, the checkout girl with the blond streaks really looked at me. Well, she didn't actually see me, didn't look at my face, but her glance, or so it seemed to me, took in my entire figure, gauging the extent of my desperation.

Even during the day, I was casually looking out for the cat after my walk on the beach, but I didn't see her. As evening came on I had to force myself not to set out too early—for a cat! And then I was a couple of minutes early after all.

There was no sign of the cat.

I went back again and reached the mailbox at about eight. I raised and dropped its flap two or three times, hoping she would hear the clatter.

The cat did not turn up.

Then I went back to my room and tried the same trick as I had played on the cat the previous day. I remember that moment as if I were seeing myself from the outside, through someone else's eyes: a man of forty in a checked shirt, wearing a shabby leather jacket and a faded hat, standing outside his door in the evening in an empty street, holding an Opinel knife and a glass ashtray, trying to entice a nameless cat by making a ringing sound . . .

Then it happened. I don't remember how much time had passed since I had been standing outside the door holding the ashtray. I was lying on my bed. I remember straightening up and—following a sudden decision—searching my little yellow dictionary for the Spanish word for *cat*. I remember sitting on the edge of the bed, holding the pages of the dictionary at a diagonal angle in the candlelight, and among the abbreviations typical of dictionaries the one magical word leaped out: *gata*.

Cabo de Gata: I am on the Cape of the Cat, I thought.

I remember that I truly felt the scales fall from my eyes—an expression I had taken to be a mere manner of speaking. The air around me seemed to become more transparent, the items flickering in the candlelight clearer. The dead cat, the living cat. The dream of resurrection . . . The fact that my mother's hair had only been dyed red simply served as added confirmation. How else would she have appeared to me? Gray? As a gray tabby cat? Would I have recognized her then? And at that moment of great clarity I knew what she had wanted to tell me, and that it couldn't have been said better, more cogently, or not with the means available to a cat—perhaps it couldn't be said more cogently at all, for the words in which I wrote it down later seemed to me a very poor paraphrase of the cat's message, and the poverty of my words seemed to be a part of that message in itself, as indeed did every wonderful, deceptive, precise detail of the incident. My purchase of cat food. My ridiculous attempt at animal training with the ringing glass of an ashtray . . .

2

Put into words, the cat's message was that I was wasting my time here. That what I hoped for wasn't going to happen, and wasn't going to happen *because* I hoped for it.

I remember wandering around the streets of Cabo de Gata, secretly keeping an eye open for her. I looked at the world from her point of view. I checked the opportunities for flight on the promenade, which was populated by dogs. I saw my landlady swipe at a cat with her scrubbing brush. I thought of the charred body in the desert—and distrusted everyone.

Then I meet Alfredo on the beach. He mops his forehead with his arm. His hands are smeared with oil. He explains why his boat isn't lying on the waterline; the engine is too heavy, and he is shifting it a little farther forward. It occurs to me that oil could also be poured over a cat. Alfredo says that to shift the engine forward he would need to extend the propeller shaft. But then, he tells me, the tank won't fit in the stern of the boat. However, if he moves the tank to the bows, the boat will be in a worse position than ever on the waterline . . .

Mucho trabajo, I say. And Alfredo very seriously replies: *Poco pescado.*

I talk to Paco. He is the youngest of the brothers, but is already completely bald. His eyes are blue, the blue of the cat food can. Paco wants to know what I'm always busy writing about. I try to explain that I am keeping a diary (for some time now, in fact, I have been using my exercise books to write myself notes). As I don't know what the Spanish for *diary* is, I say I am writing down what I do every day.

But you don't do anything, replies Paco.

Paco is carefree. Paco is cheerful. Paco can write his name (as he immediately demonstrates by writing it in my exercise book). He has a beautiful wife who carries her full belly ahead of her. As we sit on the bench he feeds one of the little spotted mongrel dogs—and is gleeful when it chases a cat over the promenade, yapping at the top of its voice.

The middle brother is called Carlos. He stands behind the bar in the restaurant drawing himself a beer. I ask him why he wears a picture of Che Guevara on his chest. He likes the look of it, he says: *¡Muy bonito!* I ask him whether he knew that Guevara was a Communist. He vehemently disputes that fact. Che Guevara, he says, was a good man and fought for the poor people of the world, but he wasn't a Communist! I ask whether he has anything against Communists. He thinks about it and then says no, not really. He just has something against cats and rats: *¡Gatos y ratas!*

Then he laughs at me, with a foam mustache on his upper lip.

I feel sure that the big-bottomed girl hates cats, if only because, as it turns out, she is married to Carlos. And the silent bartender certainly doesn't like cats. But I also suspect the nun-like baker's wife, who still hands my daily *pan integral* over the counter with a gesture like a blessing, of disliking cats, perhaps for reasons of hygiene.

As for the priest, who is ahead of me in the bakery one day, the mere way he blows his nose, together with his noisy breathing, and the little Jesus pendant on the key ring that dangles out of his velvety green cassock are enough to make me think him capable of murdering cats.

I remember the long detours I made from then on when I left the bar with the billiards table, I remember the wider and wider circles in which I walked on the way home. I remember, as if the place consisted only of them, strange expanses of uncultivated wasteland with trodden earth paths running through them, sparse brushwood, unused, dusty corners, rusty climbing frames on a patch overgrown with tall grass: I remember places frequented by cats. Places where the cats of Cabo de Gata led a shadowy life, a life verging on invisibility.

They came out of hiding at night. Yes, I admit that I myself was sometimes out and about by night, or at least late in the evening, looking for the ginger tabby cat. I clattered the flap of the mailbox, I allowed myself to go the long way around on my way home over the wasteland, I hummed "The Star-Spangled Banner" when I saw the gray shadows near the trash cans because I hoped she might recognize my voice. In short, I acted like an idiot. I acted as you do only when you are in love.

I remember the attacks of malice that came over me on these nocturnal walks. Yes, I felt a perverse pleasure in observing myself on my absurd excursions. Wasn't it clear the cat wasn't coming back? Hadn't that been exactly what the message meant? She wasn't turning up because I hoped she would. I couldn't find her because I was looking for her. Nothing happened because I was always doing something. Because I was still convinced something depended on me. Because I was still hoping I could force release into being.

It was like the hag stones. The idea came to me as I was walking toward the sea coffin in the afternoon: you never found a hag stone by persistently searching in one place! I remember how I flung myself on the ground and began poking about among the pebbles in front of my nose, to prove that you never find a hag stone that way—and then I did. I found a hag stone! Furious, I threw it into the sea. I wasn't going to be given the runaround anymore. I must stop it! Stop searching. Stop waiting. Stop hoping.

That evening I stayed at home. And I did not fall for the excuses I used in trying to trick myself—ingenious double negatives leading me to think, for instance, that I must set out to prove I wasn't looking for anything, or that if I meant it seriously, I must throw away the cat food can, which was still standing like a monument on the lopsided little wardrobe. I stayed at home—*home,* what a term for it! I stayed in my room, three by three meters. I remember lying on my bed. Staring at the blue can of cat food; realizing—a little late in the day—that a song was going through my head.

It was a silly little children's rhyme, about the pug who came

into the kitchen, one of those texts in the form of an endless loop—
everyone presumably knows one of them—and this one runs:

> *Pug went into the kitchen*
> *to steal an egg or two.*
> *The cook picked up his ladle*
> *and with it Pug he slew.*
> *Pug's friends and Pug's relations,*
> *seeing him drop down dead,*
> *put up a gravestone to him,*
> *and on the stone it said:*
> *Pug went into the kitchen . . .*

And so on and so forth, over and over again.

I listened for a while. I don't recollect whether I was singing
it in my head or really singing aloud. I listened and marveled, as
you sometimes do marvel at something you know only too well,
thinking: how simple but how effective. You couldn't get out of the
loop, I thought with something close to satisfaction, you had to go
back to the beginning again and again . . . *Pug's friends and Pug's
relations . . . and on the stone it said* . . . And again . . . and then . . .

No, now I catch myself out in attempted deception. In fact, I
don't now remember how it happened. I don't even know whether it
happened at night or in the morning. I only remember the striking
idea that suddenly came into in my mind and, put into words, could
run: if I stop hoping, it is only because I hope that what I hope for
will happen because I've stopped hoping for it.

But presumably I never thought it out like that. Presumably it
crept up on me, like all ideas, in preverbal form. And presumably—
this also comes closest to my recollection—it appeared on the surface
of my conscious mind, with the typical, incalculable delay of such
ideas, as a single word.

And the word was: TRAP.

3

I remember that the sea was very calm.

I remember that Paco chugged past me in his green-and-white boat a little way from the shore, and waved.

I remember that there was chickpea soup that day.

I remember the sense of utter helplessness (which, curiously enough, I connect with the chickpeas, which don't slip down very well).

But I also remember a kind of pride. As if it were a distinction that this should happen to me, of all people.

And then again there were entirely different factors: I am standing before my American friend's coffin in silence, not singing. The sea breeze cools the sweat on my brow. I am sweating because of the hopelessness of my situation. No, it's not a joke, not an exercise in writing. It is not material for a novel . . .

Then something else happens—the day before that, or the day after it? I think I remember that it was the day before, and that it struck me as a bad omen: the woman with the plaster cast on her leg appears—without the plaster cast. She strides along the promenade, her head held high. Then I see that she has made up her face. She has done something, heaven knows what, to her hair; has waved or permed it. This new woman walks past me, giving me a cool greeting over her shoulder. I must add that she had recently begun talking to me. She had stopped by my bench, had told me her troubles, I suppose about her accident—to be honest, I hadn't understood what she was saying, but did that matter?

I am not playing billiards now. Instead, I sit beside one of the salt-water lakes in the afternoon, watching the flamingos until I feel sure that they are mechanical toys, wound up regularly by the bird warden.

I count my money back in my room. I count my money and work out that if I go on in the same way I can survive for another seventy-three days here. And I count the days I have already spent here and work out that it has been seventy-three days! What does that mean? I do several addition and subtraction sums. I add up the digits in a number. I look for the nearest prime number. I work out when the cat came . . . when the American came, when the Englishman came . . . I begin writing numbers in my exercise book. I try deciphering the numerical sequence. I try Fibonacci numbers. I try to find a formula, some kind of regularity, some sense in it all.

Then I am back on the promenade. There is a starry sky above me; it is evening. I walk, trying not to think of numbers anymore. I take the first right turn, toward the mailbox—I take it automatically. Then she leaps out of a doorway, obviously a movement of flight. But as she leaps, so my memory tells me, anyway within fractions of a second, before I know it, she stops in midmovement, turns, and mews at me.

To this day I wonder how cats really recognize us. By our smell—within fractions of a second? By our faces—in the dark? By our stature—spotted out of the corner of an eye as the cat leaps? In this case, particularly when our acquaintanceship wasn't a long one.

She follows me as she did that first evening. I leave the doors open. I take the can of cat food down from the wardrobe and open it with shaking fingers. I scrape out a helping with my Opinel knife—how much can a cat digest at a single meal?—and put it in the glass ashtray.

She eats.

The tip of her tail quivers.

The soft snarl of a beast of prey comes from her jaws.

Maybe it is because of that sound—the rasping snarl of a beast of prey—that I call her a little lioness. Not because my mother was proud of her star sign, Leo. My mother, I say, was the big lioness. You are the little lioness. That is the first thing I say to her.

I remember how she begins exploring the room: cautiously, without a sound. She keeps low on the floor, looks under the beds, under the wardrobe.

I remember how—briefly examining her destination, getting her back paws into position—she jumps up to the sill of the little bathroom window, high on the wall, looking out on the inner courtyard. Yes, I knew cats could jump well—but what elegance . . .

I don't like the way she sniffs around the opposite bed; after all, she is a half-wild animal, maybe she roams around the trash cans in the night, perhaps she has fleas . . . I warn her off in an undertone. She immediately jumps off the bed—and has gone.

I swear to myself never to warn her off again. Not to try training her to do as I want. To accept her as she is. *If she comes back again.*

And she does come back again. I meet her by the mailbox at eight in the evening. No earlier! I do look for her casually during the day, casually, but always in vain: our date is for the evening, by the mailbox. And it stays that way to the end, the bitter end.

I remember how she begins rubbing around my legs, her tail held high, fleetingly, not quite concentrating. I remember the first time I stroke her, awkwardly, as movements carried out for the first time tend to be: I hold out my hand, and she rubs her head or the sides of her mouth against it, then walks on under the palm of my hand until her erect tail seems to act as an obstacle that she wants to overcome . . . and although of course I don't seriously allow myself to think she is my mother, what we are doing strikes me as slightly incestuous.

And then there is her purring! Every child knows that a cat purrs. Even I, and I had hardly any contact with cats before her (my father was against keeping animals in the house), knew that a cat purrs. But I always thought the purr came somehow, I don't know how, from deep inside the cat. In fact, it is bound up with the animal's breathing; she purrs as she breathes in and out, and even if the note seems to be regular at first (indeed you get the impression that the

cat is trying to keep it regular), if you listen carefully there is a difference between the purr as she breathes in and as she breathes out,
and again, if you listen, you can tell the point at which the cat, so to
speak, switches into reverse gear.

I also notice that she can adjust her long whiskers. She lays them
against her cheeks when she is walking past my hand, and raises
them again when she has stopped walking.

She can move her ears. She listens. When she is unsure of something she flattens her ears.

Her eyes are green—in fact, exactly the color of my mother's eyes:
a dark mineral green with brown specks. When the pupils narrow
to vertical slits, she looks slightly dangerous, like a robot. Strangely,
they can narrow to slits even when she is most relaxed—then the cat
blinks at me as if to convince me of her innocence.

How do cats drink? After a while that question occurs to me. They
must drink, after all, but how? I have no idea. I cut the base off a plastic bottle, fill it with water, and put it down for her. Sure enough—she
drinks! She drinks (presumably like all animals) by dipping her tongue
into the water and lapping the liquid up in quick, rhythmical movements. I sit on the edge of my bed, listening and counting: she laps
four times running. Sometimes she loses count and laps five times.

After a while—after three, five, or seven days—I cautiously
close the door at night. She accepts that. She jumps up on the other
bed, sits down, and tucks her forepaws under her. She purrs. Soon
the candles have burned down. There is only purring in the room,
warm, happy purring.

4

She leaves me at seven every morning. I stay in bed for another half an hour, and then I go to bathe. As there is never anyone on the promenade at this time of day, I decided one day to replace a cold shower in the morning by bathing in the sea.

Then comes my usual walk to the bakery. The nun-like baker's wife blesses me with a *pan integral,* and I put a coin in the Jesus collection box.

I make myself a coffee: the señora—as I call her, although by now I have grasped the fact that she is generally known as the widow (*la viuda*)—has been letting me make my own coffee for some time. In a portentous cackle like a chicken's, rising from the depths, she explained what I must take care to do (all I remember about it is that an indicator had to be in the green area shown on the machine). With a couple of hefty taps—*knock-knock!*—I eject the old coffee grounds from the funnel (they are baked hard like an ice-hockey puck), and as coffee streams into the container I spread my *pan integral,* or rather dribble olive oil on it in order to eat half of it as soon as the fresh coffee has run through the funnel (keeping the other half for evening). I eat it with a tomato that the señora places on the counter in a small saucer for me.

If the señora isn't looking I refrain from foaming the milk. She likes people to foam the milk. I think she wants everyone to appreciate everything her wonderful coffee machine can do.

After breakfast I sit on my bench with my second cup of coffee. The sun shines. I am still overcome by a strange optimism as I sit there. I feel very close to achieving insight.

There is still too much movement. My mind is still uneasy. My mood still changes too often. But I have a presentiment. I begin to have some idea of the true message of the cat.

Are all cats like that?

You could set your watch by her. All our rituals, once we have worked them out, take place in the same way and observe the same sequence: feeding, stroking. Then comes the time for purring. At some point in the night, when I am asleep, she moves to settle on my feet. If I wake up, then I find it hard to drop off to sleep again, because I hardly dare move; I want her to stay there.

The observations that I make in the morning are increasingly microscopic. There is nothing much more to notice. Nothing new happens. The last change was the disappearance of the woman with the plaster cast. Paco appeared instead, and was a good substitute.

I don't mean Paco the fisherman but old Paco. Probably some member of the family, a city dweller. At least, he is not from these parts, as anyone can tell because he never goes out of the house in his slippers. He wears black shoes, not very new but always well polished. He sits in front of the restaurant in a white plastic chair near the door. Sitting there, he sings a few bars of flamenco now and then in a voice rusty with age—flamenco in its purest, most original form. He sighs heavily. Existential melancholy. He sings whatever comes into his head. I wish I knew what it is.

Perhaps his wife has just died? Perhaps he was one of the Franco regime's thugs and is now looking back at the old days, feeling half-contrite, half-bitter?

Then Paco falls silent again. Sits in the sun, saying nothing. Now and then the shouts of the women helping the señora to prepare lunch come from the kitchen. And when, after a while, Paco raises his voice again I understand that he is simply repeating words, scraps of sentences, indiscriminately and at random, just as they reach his ear from the kitchen.

A few tables have been placed outside the restaurant. I eat outdoors now, with a view of the sea. It is hard to tell whether that annoys the big-bottomed girl or not. She takes as little notice of me as ever. Bangs my plate down, turns, presenting me, as she lasciviously undulates away, with the mighty mechanism of her backside.

The salad and the main course are always the same, but the soup changes from day to day—however, as I have now come to realize, these changes have their own method and rules. On Monday the soup is made from the remains of Sunday's paella. On Tuesday there is chicken soup, on Wednesday chickpea soup, on Thursday vegetable soup with large and carelessly peeled cloves of garlic in it, and on Friday, I think, fish soup. I don't remember Saturday's soup, and on Sunday there is no soup, but paella instead.

I am positively delighted by this realization, as if I had discovered a new natural constant. I remember the phrase *cosmic soup,* and it passes through my mind as a collective term, so to speak, for the weekly sequence of soups. The main course is always fish, and after once trying in vain to revise the decision I made on what I would drink, I am secretly glad that the big-bottomed girl ignores or perhaps has simply forgotten my new request, that she still puts a bottle of red wine down on the table for me—and I refrain from reminding her.

So I drink red wine with fish. To keep my napkin from blowing away in the wind, I wedge it under the salt and pepper stand. I squeeze lemon over the nameless fish that is served every day. And I wonder whether I shall ever eat as well again.

Then comes the afternoon lull. I get through it by going for walks. The changes in the sea close to the shore from one day to the next are just within the bounds of what I can tolerate. I have to protect myself from destructive thoughts, or indeed from thinking at all. Because I understood, some time ago, that the great design, the overarching form in which past and present are wonderfully interlinked, the tone of voice in which my story is telling itself, cannot be invented, are not the work of reason, not a matter of intelligence, but—and *this,* I think, is the cat's true message—but will appear as soon as absolute equilibrium has been achieved. As soon as the world stops disturbing me by changing.

I sing "The Star-Spangled Banner." Or rather, I hum its tune.

Billiards at four. The *click-click* of the balls touching each other. In the background, the music to which extraterrestrials dance on the TV screen.

I sit on the bench to watch the sunset.

Eight o'clock: the cat's time. I feed her, I stroke her.

And then, before going to sleep, I read *El País*.

It is still the same issue, the edition of February 17, if I remember correctly. I read until my eyes close. Until the cat comes to sit on my feet. And one evening, when the light is out, when the cat is purring, when my head, when the room, when the world are all nothing but a great black purr, I have the feeling that time—at last—is standing still.

5

When I think back, it is a mystery to me that I could have overlooked the signs.

Of course spring does not arrive as ostentatiously in the desert as in Central Europe. It slinks in, bending low, it does not make a great show of splendor, but it leaves traces. Didn't I see them? Yes, I did, I remember. For instance, I remember the sudden sprinkling of yellow flowers in the desert.

The sun now is rising about a minute earlier every day—I even measured it—and sets about a minute later. Slowly, the moment when it meets the horizon in the evening is shifting, and soon, I can tell, the red sunset light will glow not over the sea but farther westward, above the mainland.

Snow still shines on the peaks of the distant Sierra Nevada, but the nights down here lost their terrors long ago. The number of candles that I burn in the evening has been reduced to one, and I light it not for warmth but for, let's say, the comfortable look of its flame.

It is true that the sky is almost always blue, and the cumulus clouds that sometimes pass can convey a sense of timelessness if you lie on your back on the beach. But it cannot be denied that cloudy days disturb the equilibrium now and then, and there was that storm in which the American disappeared.

Once a mighty wall of clouds comes up from Africa. It approaches so fast over the water that it frightens me. Then the sky grows dark, and there is a sudden smell of diesel all around.

Once it rains. Not what you would call rain by Central European standards, not enough of it to form a puddle. But the people immediately brought out their umbrellas, as if they were glad of a reason to use them once a year.

And yes, the people are here! The ghost town gradually fills up. They come here at least on weekends, not to swim yet but to eat: people from the countryside around, locals who in spite of what to me are summer temperatures stay in the dim light of the restaurant— until one Sunday a couple is suddenly sitting at "my" table outside the restaurant.

When they have eaten, the people *promenade,* literally: for an hour or so the promenade of Cabo de Gata is full of people in their Sunday best, chatting, walking up and down in little groups, even going along the promenade and back, and doing it more than once if its eight hundred paved meters aren't long enough for them.

On Monday, however, that's all over, and the street cleaner arrives, a stoic who walks erect, picking up scraps of paper from the paving stones with a long gripper while more garbage is blown along behind him, coming out of the yellow trash cans as the wind lifts their lids.

I remember all that. I saw all that, and more; I have just remembered the beach-cleaning monster, a device as large as a combine harvester (I've never seen anything like it on the Baltic coast), that one day, it could have been at the end of March, begins combing the beach beyond the promenade with a great roar (and leaves an unnatural pattern of stripes behind it). I saw all that without seeing it, I heard it without hearing it, I was amused (by the rain) or annoyed (by the beach-cleaning monster) without actually taking it in until the day when I discovered the cat was pregnant.

Or do you say "in kitten" with cats?

Oddly enough, I don't remember the moment of my discovery; I have no visual image of it. What I remember when I think of discovering her pregnancy is mainly my own hysteria; the few seconds in which all kinds of horrific scenarios passed through my mind—the idea of a cat giving birth under my bed, of six blind, bloodstained kittens, their shit, their mewing. I already imagined myself lining a vegetable crate with old rags, in case the cat had her kittens in my room (but how was I to make her understand that she was to have them in the crate lined with rags?), while at the same time I thought of the scandal when it was discovered I was harboring a litter of kittens in my room.

I forgot to mention that soon after the cat's arrival I began cleaning my own room, a job the big-bottomed girl was originally supposed to do, and I had ascribed her bad temper to that, not that she was any better tempered once I began cleaning it myself (in fact, she seemed to bear me a grudge for relieving her of the task!)—anyway, I had begun doing it mainly because I was afraid the cat might pee in my room in the night (which of course she never did). And once my hysterical reaction to the discovery of her pregnancy had died down, I told myself the cat would not give birth to a litter of bloodstained kittens under my bed either. She would do it all as cleverly and circumspectly as she had done everything else so far, and yet in a way I felt as if she had gone behind my back.

Suddenly the cat's behavior seemed to me rational, almost calculating. Her bold approach to me, her regular appearance in the evening, her pleased response when I rubbed the back of her neck, even her purring, and her dark, bewitching gaze, suddenly struck me as insultingly deliberate. It was the Darwinian constant: her behavior served to protect the species. Everything she did was done for the good of the young in her belly—it was as simple, as shatteringly simple, as that.

I remember that next morning (or perhaps it was the morning after that, or even two mornings later) I caught the bus and went to Almería. I hadn't decided to leave Cabo de Gata for good, or not yet, but the monotony of my life there had now, after my return to the temporal scale of things, suddenly become intolerable. Although of course I knew I was being unjust in blaming the cat—as if I had taken that monotony on myself for her sake. I remember that her impatient mewing began to annoy me; I even thought I heard an undertone of reproach if I did not immediately reach for the can of cat food as soon as we were in my room. It felt like an imposition that I had to keep still when she came to sit on my feet at night. I began to sneer at her for failing to realize that however often she tried scratching a closed door when she wanted it to open, it was no good.

I remember spending a confused day in Almería. I remember having breakfast on the Rambla (here, as in Barcelona, the city center was notable for a former riverbed); I remember the mighty fortifications on a hill; I remember the midday heat in the streets that became narrower and more dilapidated the farther uphill I went—until on the other side of the hill the city fell into genuine ruin.

I remember sitting on a shady park bench in the afternoon and cutting up a honeydew melon with my Opinel knife. I remember that a vagrant who looked like Tarzan sat down on the bench diagonally opposite me: his feet were bare, he wore furs and had matted hair, and his face was so blackened with the sun that the whites of his eyes flashed like the eyes of the coalmen you still saw in my childhood. He too began cutting something up with a large knife; I didn't like to look, but as I sat for a few moments, my hands sticky with melon juice and at a loss to do anything about it, his goblin eyes met mine, and that, together with a tiny nod of his head, drew my attention to a small drinking fountain only a few steps away.

I had meant to spend the night on the beach in Almería, to see whether I could survive the coming summer here without any fixed abode, but the suspicion that the Tarzan vagrant took me for one of his own kind—whether because of my squashed hat and my thermal mat, or did the instincts of a homeless man tell him what I was like?—made me hesitate. I looked at two hotels, one of which, formerly a grand building with dark marble floors belonging to another era, was even reasonably inexpensive. However, when I saw the iron bedstead in a room much too large for it I couldn't make up my mind to spend any of my dwindling reserves of cash on a night there.

Half to compensate myself for not doing so, half out of desperation, I ordered grilled lamb cutlets—after three months of fish—in a handsome street restaurant at the far end of an avenue lined with palm trees. I remember having some difficulty in getting a table; all the seats were occupied. This seemed to be the time when the Spanish ate their evening meal. But just as the Spanish visitors to Cabo de Gata stood up almost at the same time after eating, as if by tacit agreement, and went out on the promenade, here they also rose to their feet with determination after their meal and disappeared—where to? By the time my cutlets were served, I found myself the only guest sitting in the light of the streetlamps.

I remember the relaxed mood in the background, the laughter of the waiters, the soft music (Elvis Presley), and I remember that a young woman with the look of a gypsy in thin, almost transparent clothes stared at me from the entrance of a building, like a hungry dog wanting the bones of my lamb cutlets. Suddenly—devouring the meat, my fingers greasy—I felt rich, or more precisely I thought I knew what it was like to be rich, or even more precisely I thought for a few moments that I felt the lowest, least edifying satisfaction of the rich, which consisted of knowing that others are not rich, that there are poor people whose lives draw your attention to your own wealth, and although I felt bad about even being capable of such sentiments, I was tempted once again to spend some of my little remaining money on a night in that old and once grand hotel—but then there was the sum that would have been necessary for the realization of my still indistinct fantasies. They were somehow bound up with the iron bedstead, the dark marble floors, and the bones that I was gnawing now.

So I went down to the beach and sought out a place to sleep between two rowboats.

6

I went back to Cabo de Gata on foot, a walk of about twenty-five kilometers (or was it thirty? I could Google it), keeping to the seashore all the way. A bus ticket wouldn't have been expensive, so I wasn't saving much, but I also wanted to prove to myself that my feet would carry me in an emergency. And they did carry me, although I must admit that it seemed like a long way.

I had slept badly; there had been an astonishing number of people on the beach, talking and drinking sparkling wine (or maybe I only imagined that last bit). Later I had reluctantly eavesdropped on a pair of lovers lying between two nearby boats, and then I had lain awake for a long time, afraid of being discovered. I felt uncomfortable about being taken for either a vagrant or a Peeping Tom. Not until the first light of dawn did I fall asleep, and then I woke, with my hat over my eyes, only when the sun was high in the sky.

I walked all day. I remember that I had a headache when the bay of Cabo de Gata finally appeared in the distance. An hour later I was walking—and I still recall the comfortable feeling of solid ground underfoot after so many kilometers of sand—along the familiar large paving stones of the promenade, skirting the rectangular flower beds full of succulent plants from which the stoic street cleaner used to pick out scraps of paper in vain on Fridays. The old señora was just closing the concertina-like grating, which always stuck, in front of the door. The skewbald dogs were running around in the evening sunlight, silent and placid as a shoal of fish.

I was at the mailbox promptly at eight. I remember the reproachful mew with which the cat shot out of a doorway, and how she followed me at the usual distance, or rather I remember that it suddenly seemed to me strange, almost like a pretense, that she moved along close to the ground on all fours.

As there was no cat food left, I shared the last of my manchego cheese with her, and would almost have given my own share to the hungry mother-to-be. After all, I myself had taught her to rely on me. I didn't, however, although I remember that as I dropped off to sleep, or at least at the time when the cat sat on my feet and I could feel the soft movements of the unborn kittens inside her, I resolved to look after the cat until she had had her litter and they were past the helpless stage. I wanted to be able to give myself the credit for this little good deed done in secret.

The next day everyone greeted me; they all asked where I had been: Alfredo and Carlos, and old Paco as well. As I entered the bar, even the silent bartender (who by this time, I must admit, had stopped putting a little tube of sugar and a cookie on my saucer) made a sound that could have been interpreted as a greeting, or at least as an acknowledgment that he had noticed my two days' absence.

I went back to my daily routine, or rather I tried to do so. However, my memory provides me with very few images from this period.

What I do remember is that the people coming and going on the promenade got on my nerves, so I often avoided my usual bench and went off into the desert with my thermal mat. However, I never missed lunch—on the contrary; as my cash began running out I depended on eating every last scrap of what was served. I remember suffering a positive attack of greed; I began eating "systematically," with little pauses, to make sure I got all three courses inside me (I didn't want the old señora thinking she could give me a smaller helping the next day!), and so I never missed lunch. However, I didn't play billiards as often, and if I did it was usually against the silent bartender whose name, I think, was also Paco, and whose dangling gold chain, as I remember, was never at rest as he leaned far over the billiards table while calculating a complicated maneuver.

My walks also became more irregular, both in the distance I covered and in their frequency, and if I did once go as far as the metal container that I had called "the coffin," I don't recollect ever humming "The Star-Spangled Banner" again; indeed, I think that as I stood there looking out to sea, it struck me as peculiar that I had ever done such a thing.

I don't remember anything else.

Or rather, of course, I remember sitting in the little café on the promenade, the one that was back in business now that the summer season was here. I remember meeting all sorts of people in the café as time went on, tourists and local inhabitants alike. I remember the usual conversations—where do you come from, what are you doing here? And I remember that once, on a Sunday, I took a day off from the cat and accepted the invitation of a Canadian (I think they were Canadian) couple who had rented a large, two-story holiday villa in Cabo de Gata. I remember the congenial party they gave, the animated mishmash of English and Spanish that we spoke, a remarkably virtuoso performance by a flamenco guitarist with the figure and hands of a boxer, who drank nothing but canned Dutch beer, which he claimed was the best in the world, and I remember that the waiter with three days' growth of beard, whom I had seen serving burning-hot sausages in the promenade café, handed around photos of his oil paintings, which measured four by three meters. And I remember that everything seemed to me very far away, that although I was in fact there I felt a longing to be there myself.

On all other days I went to the mailbox punctually at eight and met the cat, until the time—ten or twelve or fourteen days later—when the accident, as I now call it, happened.

I remember how she was stretching on the other bed, showing her stomach so that you already almost *saw* her kittens as they moved; I remember my irresistible longing to touch the pale, soft, downy fur on her belly—and not just touch it; my feet already knew what the kittens' movements felt like, and I wanted to feel them with my hands as well.

The cat gently fended me off with her paw, but I was not to be deterred. I thought it was my right, after all my care of her, after such a long time, after so many cans of cat food brought back from the supermarket with a sense of embarrassment. I thought that, as the foster father of the unborn kittens, so to speak, I had a right to touch her pregnant belly, and I held her paw, gently at first and then more firmly as her resistance grew. The cat mewed twice. And then it happened.

Today, twenty years later (and I have had cats of my own for a long time), I know what a cat's claws can do. So I know that what she did to me then was hardly more than a scratch, probably just the reflex action that can sometimes be induced in cats if you stroke their bellies. She had warned me twice. And she had spared me. And I have probably suppressed, out of shame, exactly what happened in the next few seconds. Did I hit her? Did I throw her off the bed?

I remember that the cat made a sound, and it seemed dangerous. Then I see her jumping up on the sill of the little bathroom window, despite her bulky pregnancy—and she was gone.

For three or four days I went to the mailbox in the evening, once even taking the can of cat food. I walked around the wasteland until well into the night. I spoke from a distance to the shadows that appeared on the outlines of the trash cans. I walked up and down the streets, trying to banish the thought that I might have killed six kittens.

Finally I tipped everything left in the can of cat food into the glass ashtray and put it on the windowsill outside my room.

I remember lying across my bed, turned to the window, my feet on the mattress of the bed opposite. It seems to me that I lay like that all night, watching the shadowy outlines that appeared silently on the other side of the window. Cats seemed to find the proximity of the food to the house suspect. They appeared only briefly, ate in haste, looking again and again at the flickering candlelight in my room—and disappeared once more. I remember a thin black-and-white cat; today I would say he was a tom with half his tail missing who had already met me once on the wasteland; a handsomely patterned tortoiseshell diva wearing a collar (were there really people in Cabo de Gata who kept cats as pets?); a totally black cat whose sparkling eyes were all that I could see; a young gray tabby like the one on the label of the cat food can; finally a ginger tabby, but with a white-tipped tail, and even without that I would have known it wasn't my ginger tabby.

Not *that* cat. Not the one after whom, if it hadn't already had a name, I would call the place where I spent a hundred and twenty-three days trying to write a novel.

7

I know it would be cleverer to end the book at once, instead of changing if not its style at least its animal species. It would be better to let the story close with a few fine-sounding, quotable comments, comforting sayings about cats, about life (for instance, that it is not a good idea to try stroking the stomach of a female in kitten—combining life and cats in a principle with a proverbial sound to it). And no doubt it would be wise to keep the image with which my stay in the village concludes for another occasion.

But I have resolved to let myself be guided by what I remember in writing this story, so this last memory of Cabo de Gata should come at the end of it.

The story ends on the following Saturday.

I know it was a Saturday because that was the day of the fish market. There hadn't been any fish market in the winter months, but now half the village went down to the beach, where the fishermen offered their fresh wares, usually still alive, for sale straight from the orange-colored crates in which they were carried ashore.

I remember walking around among the boats. It was still early in the morning, the light was bright and cast harsh shadows on the trodden sand. People argued about quantities and prices. Fish were weighed, put in plastic bags, bills and coins made their way into old tin cans.

I remember all that only vaguely, however, like a film without a sound track. Even the image that I remember so clearly is silent.

It shows a small ray, obviously not worth anything, left lying unnoticed in one of the brightly colored fishing boats, in a little puddle of seawater that had formed between the wooden ribs at the bottom of the boat. The puddle was shallow, just deep enough to cover the ray. Its freedom of movement was practically zero; the water wasn't deep enough for it to turn over, and the creature lay there upside down.

I had never seen the underside of a ray before. Its belly was white. Its eyes must have been on its other side, and only a small, toothless mouth could be seen gasping for air in something like the rhythm of a human heartbeat.

Then the mouth suddenly stopped moving. After a few seconds the little creature writhed once, briefly, as if it were trying to turn over—and died.

And then what?

Then nothing. It died. And I packed my things and caught the morning bus, although the weekly price that I had already paid would have included that day's lunch.

(Written between November 2011 and August 2012)

Eugen Ruge was born in the Urals, studied mathematics in Berlin, and became a member of the research staff at the Central Institute for Geophysics in Potsdam. Before leaving the GDR for the West in 1988 he was a writer, contributing to documentaries made at the state-owned DEFA Studios. Since 1989 he has been writing and translating for theaters and broadcasters, and he teaches periodically at the Berlin University of the Arts. In 2011, he came to international acclaim when he won the German Book Prize for *In Times of Fading Light,* his debut novel, which went on to be translated into more than twenty languages. He lives in Berlin.

Anthea Bell is a freelance translator from German and French. Her translations include works of fiction and general nonfiction, books for young people, and classics by E. T. A. Hoffmann, Freud, Kafka, and Stefan Zweig. She has won a number of translation awards in the United Kingdom and the United States.

The text of Cabo de Gata is set in Adobe Garamond Pro. Book design by Connie Kuhnz. Composition by Bookmobile Design and Publishing Services, Minneapolis, Minnesota. Manufactured by Versa Press on acid-free, 30 percent postconsumer wastepaper.